ALSO BY ELIE WIESEL

A Mad Desire to Dance

The Time of the Uprooted

The Judges

Night

Dawn

The Accident

The Town Beyond the Wall

The Gates of the Forest

The Jews of Silence

Legends of Our Time

A Beggar in Jerusalem

One Generation After

Souls on Fire

The Oath

Ani Maamin (cantata)

Zalmen, or The Madness of God (play)

Messengers of God

A Jew Today

Four Hasidic Masters

The Trial of God (play)

The Testament

Five Biblical Portraits

Somewhere a Master

The Golem
(illustrated by Mark Podwal)

The Fifth Son

Against Silence
(edited by Irving Abrahamson)

Twilight

The Six Days of Destruction
(with Albert Friedlander)

A Journey into Faith
(conversations with John Cardinal O'Connor)

From the Kingdom of Memory

Sages and Dreamers

The Forgotten

A Passover Haggadah
(illustrated by Mark Podwal)

All Rivers Run to the Sea

Memory in Two Voices
(with François Mitterrand)

King Solomon and His Magic Ring
(illustrated by Mark Podwal)

And the Sea Is Never Full

Conversations with Elie Wiesel
(with Richard D. Heffner)

THE SONDERBERG CASE

ELIE WIESEL

Translated from the French
by Catherine Temerson

ALFRED A. KNOPF NEW YORK 2010

THE SONDERBERG CASE

A NOVEL

THIS IS A BORZOI BOOK
PUBLISHED BY ALFRED A. KNOPF

www.aaknopf.com

Library of Congress Cataloging-in-Publication Data
Wiesel, Elie, [date]
[Cas Sonderberg. English]
The Sonderberg case: a novel / Elie Wiesel ; translated from the French by Catherine Temerson.—1st American ed.
p. cm.
"This is a Borzoi book."
"Originally published in France as Le cas Sonderberg by Éditions Grasset & Fasquelle, Paris, in 2008"—T.p. verso.
ISBN 978-0-307-27220-1
I. Temerson, Catherine. II. Title.
PQ2683.I32C3713 2010 843'.914—dc22 2009038525

Manufactured in the United States of America
First American Edition

For Shira, Elijah, and their parents—
with tenderness

THE SONDERBERG CASE

MUST ONE SUFFER and then feel death's ice-cold breath on the nape of one's neck in order to understand why one has been going around since earliest childhood with an ill-defined despondency close to melancholy?

I felt it long before the trial.

And afterward.

I felt it on the day Dr. Feldman explained to me, in a gentle, slow voice, as though he were addressing a child, that the body can become our implacable enemy.

One day, I thought, I'll turn it into a novel.

Concerning the trial, I had long been convinced that I'd never know the truth of what really happened that day between the two men, blood relations, in the high mountains of the Adirondacks.

Accident? Suicide? Murder? Can one willingly take to the grave an enigma that refuses to disclose its secret?

What evil spirit had driven Werner Sonderberg to take a break from his classes at New York University and leave town for a trip so far from the Village with the aged, disillusioned relative said to be his uncle? Yedidyah wondered. What could they have said to each other for their quarrel to reach a pitch of deadly violence? And who was this uncle whose tragic death, far from anyone, loomed over the Manhattan courtroom filled with journalists, lawyers, and curious onlookers for days and days?

The media, absorbed by ever-changing current events, or from boredom, no longer mention the trial. The fate of an individual matters little compared to the goings-on of political, financial, and artistic celebrities. But Yedidyah thinks about it often, too often probably; in fact, he remains haunted by it. Remembered images from the trial never leave him; and the proceedings echo in his mind. The lit-up room; the jury members, whose faces were alternately impassive and horrified; the judge, who at times looked like he was dozing but never missed a word of what was being said; the prosecutor, who thought he was the avenging angel. And the defendant, oscillating between defiance and remorse, avoiding the mournful gaze of his beautiful fiancée. Sometimes, when Yedidyah assesses his work, with its setbacks and intervals of calm, his dazzling triumphs and slow or dizzying failures, this trial stands out for him like black granite attracting the twilight. Years have gone by, but Yedidyah still can't reach a verdict.

Where does a man's guilt begin and where does it end? What is definitive, irrevocable?

One thought has obsessed him constantly since then. Thanks to Dr. Feldman's diagnosis, he became conscious of his mortality: Could he possibly go, and duly leave his children, their mother, Alika, and the entire convulsive and condemned world, without *certainty*?

Until my final hour on this earth, I'll remember this event that bore me, carrying me from one discovery to another, from memory to memory, from emotion to emotion, and I'll never know the real reason behind it.

Why this meeting, this confrontation with a destiny that touched mine on the surface, like a coincidence?

I could have studied other subjects, been interested in music rather than theater; I could have had other teachers, been captivated by another woman and not fallen in love with Alika; I could have been less close to my grandfather and my uncle Méir; made other friends, cherished other ambitions—in short: I could have been born somewhere else, perhaps in the same country, the same city as Werner Sonderberg, and explored other memories. I could have lived my entire life without knowing the truth about my own origins.

I could simply have not existed, or ceased to exist. Or not been me.

I was in my office getting ready to write a review of a play that had just opened the Off Broadway season. It was *Oedipus,* an ultramodern, contemporary, hopeless (too chatty) interpretation of it.

On rereading the notes I'd taken during the performance, I wondered about the play's endurance. How could it be explained? After all, of the three hundred plays written by the three giants of ancient Greece—Aeschylus, Sophocles, and Euripides—all but around thirty have vanished. How could the selection and censorship of time be explained?

Do the gods, known and feared for their whims, have a say in this matter? Weren't they themselves subjected to the same test? Some of the plays have become popular again while others seem consigned to the so-called dustbin of history: Is there any justice in this? And what about the collective memory of artistic creation? For every Prometheus and Sisyphus haunting scholars, how many of their former equals are barely stirring and covered in dust?

And then what could possibly have induced the producer to stage a doubtless costly show that should have remained in his head or in the drawer?

I mentioned my "office" a few paragraphs ago. A tiny, unused corner in the newsroom of a New York daily. A modest worktable—a desk—and two chairs rented by two

European magazines for which I was culture correspondent in the United States. This was well before the invasion of computers. The place had all the characteristics that spring to mind when you think of a hellish environment, except that Dante's hell, with its nine circles, is surely more orderly. Unbearable racket, the incessant ringing of twenty telephones, impatient calls from the editors, the shouts of the photographers and messengers, the hot topic in the news: the arrogance of a politician, his rival's defeat, the inside story on an actress's love life, the confessions of an ideologically motivated killer, a scandal in fashionable circles or in the slums. One article is too long, the other not long enough. Headlines and subheadings compete for top billing. Two dates, two facts that can't be reconciled. A beginner is reprimanded; he breaks down in tears. An old-timer tries to console him. This, too, will pass; everything passes. In short, it's not easy to concentrate. Not to mention my immediate preoccupation: my birthday.

The fact is, I have a strong aversion to birthdays. Not other people's birthdays, but my own. Especially surprise birthday parties. I dislike planned surprises. The obligation to put on an act. To lie. To lapse into abject hypocrisy. To smile at everyone and thank the good Lord for having been born. And men for having been created in His image, though He is supposed to have everything except an image. That said, let's get back to our dear Oedipus, his complexes made famous by Freud and his conflicts with the dreadful Creon. Are they contemporary heroes? This would explain the failure of the play. Does it tell us that the world changes but not human nature? Fine, we know this, and we get used to it. The Greeks' taste for authority and power, the passion for freedom and wisdom among their philosophers, the choice between obedience and faithfulness. In our day as well? An idea that deserves further thought. And a conception of spectacle.

It was at that moment that my strange life was turned upside down, as they say.

A woman comes up to my desk. She waits for me to notice her and ask if she is looking for someone; if she is, I'm sure it can't be me.

In her forties. Attractive. Dark hair; dark eyes; serene and self-confident.

"I was told that you're the person I'm looking for," she says.

"Me?"

"Yes, you."

"But I'm not on the editorial staff anymore . . . I mean, not really."

"I know."

"I'm just a subtenant of sorts."

"I know that, too."

"So then . . ."

"You used to be a reporter."

"Yes. How do you know?"

She smiles. "You're the one who covered the trial of . . ."

"Of Werner Sonderberg. You remember that? Congratulations."

"I'd like to talk to you about it."

"After so many years?"

"Time is no matter."

"I don't understand."

"I'm Werner's wife."

Suddenly, I recognized her. I had seen her in court during the trial. The mysterious fiancée.

"He'd like to meet you."

"Right now?"

The past resurfaces. For a while, years ago, after the trial, I belonged in earnest to the journalism brotherhood—I mean the active, dynamic, and above all romantic brotherhood. People came to see me, to ask me questions, to give me leads. It was the best period in my life. The most exciting.

I supplied information and explanations. I commented on events both frivolous and historical. I talked about known people to unknown readers. I thought I was useful. Essential.

"We're here on a visit. Werner would like to see you."

I remember the trial. Not surprising. It's the only one I ever attended. The solemn setting. Seriousness, the solemn law. The tension in the room. The anonymous jurors: destiny in twelve faces. The duel between the prosecutor and the defense lawyers. And the defendant: I see him again. Impassive. A living challenge to threats of imprisonment.

Actually, I had discovered journalism well before working in the field. My uncle Méir, early on, considered it the finest profession. It is he who made me appreciate, as an adolescent, the multifaceted world refracted by news and editorials in print. He ranked the committed journalist as the equal of writers and philosophers. In his youth, at New York University, he used to go to the corner coffee shop every day to read the morning papers and sip his cappuccino. If he didn't go, it was because he was unwell or studying for an exceptionally difficult exam. He would then save press clippings for a later time. "See," he used to say to me, "there you are, sitting at your desk or lying on the bed, and without lifting a finger you find out what's happening in faraway countries. Isn't it miraculous?" He was right: no need to travel anymore in order to be informed. The reporter acts as your ears and eyes. And sometimes as your compass or alter ego.

What was it in the press that so interested him? Current events, fleeting and elusive? Political and economic editorials, usually superficial with their respectable optimism or skepticism? The sports pages? Trivial news items in which the acts are more or less the same but the names are new? He was fascinated by the present: he believed in living it to the point of exhaustion. And that, he confessed to me one day, possibly laughing under his breath, was "for purely theological reasons."

When Méir became nearly blind in his old age, one of us—I, Alika, or one of our sons—would read poetry or novels to him.

Méir had no children. To be more precise, he no longer had any. In love with his wife, Drora, a vigorous and rebellious blonde, he used to say, "She's my child." And Drora used to say of him, "He's my lunatic."

Why had he quarreled with my father? They had stopped seeing each other. Was it something about Drora? Or because of their break with family tradition? Admittedly, they were less religious than my grandparents, but was this a reason to stop being in touch?

One day, several years ago, I brought up the issue with my mother. She brushed me aside gently: "I'd rather not talk about it."

"Why not?"

"Don't ask me why."

"Is it because of me? Because I have parents and they don't have a son? Why do people refer to him as an unhappy recluse? What is his life all about?"

"Be quiet," said my mother, after turning slightly pale. "One day you'll find out."

"Through whom?"

"Maybe through him." This was when I felt for the first time that I had come upon a family secret.

My father read the newspapers, too, but not as assiduously. And my grandfather even less assiduously. "Trivial news events are the rage these days," he used to say, stressing the last words. To which he immediately added, "In the old days, major events *were*." Actually, the past interested him more than the present. Only bound books interested him. Preferably yellowed pages, coated with the dust of the ages.

Good books led him to think about the men chosen by God: he almost resented their being too famous; he would have liked to discover them and keep them all to himself. Between information and knowledge, he used to say, he had a preference for knowledge. And the latter is not found in newspapers.

My grandfather loved contemplating the mystery of transience and the influence of time on language; what seems attractive, dazzling, and profound tomorrow won't be so the day after tomorrow. All these so-called powerful and famous people, in every field, starved for glory and honors, are leading lights today, but sooner or later they are usually forgotten and sometimes despised. So what's the point of ambition?

As for my mother, her hope, of course, was that I would become a lawyer—better yet, a great lawyer. In America, of course. My older brother, Itzhak, a future businessman, predicted I would have a career as an engineer, no doubt because I spent hours as a child taking apart cheap tools and expensive watches, to the great annoyance of our parents.

So, then, how did I become a journalist?

That's another story.

The trial to which the young woman is alluding made a lasting impression on me. I wouldn't be the man I am, trailing a host of ghosts, if I hadn't been present at the deliberations with a mixture of frustration and enthusiasm.

At the time, the young Werner, accused of murder, and his burden of bloodstained memories, had exerted on me a fascination whose traces have yet to fade away. They even affected my relationship with my own family.

My father—like his father, but in a different area—a teacher of ancient literature in a Jewish high school in Manhattan, is a gentle dreamer and somewhat withdrawn. A storyteller but not talkative. I regret that he never brought up his parents' memories from the old country, nor his own as the child of survivors. Was he even familiar with them? When someone mentioned the Tragedy in his presence—it had suddenly become a subject of conversation in social circles—he withdrew into a deep silence that no one dared penetrate.

His failing? Attracted by the imaginary, he sometimes couldn't distinguish the real from lived experience. He asked himself questions by probing his fantasy with an almost painful sincerity. "Had I been one of Socrates' judges, would I have condemned him?" Or: "Had I been a colleague of Rabbi Eliezer, son of Hyrcanus, Rabbi Yehoshua's opponent, would I have voted for his banishment?" Or: "Had I lived in the Spain of Isabella the Catholic, would I have chosen conversion like Abraham Senior, or exile like Don Itzhak Abrabanel?" This tormented him. But, if you think about it, was this really a failing?

Did he imagine himself in his father's position, in that cursed time and place? Did he wonder how he would have behaved in the face of the daily trials, over there, when the whim of a killer sufficed to make an entire family or community vanish from the face of the earth?

A few more words about my grandfather, who did return from there. He didn't talk about it very much, either. Perhaps for the same reasons, or for others. He may have talked about it through his readings of and commentaries on the other great catastrophes in Jewish history, in ancient and medieval times.

With a face marked by the years, with a haunted gaze, he was handsome and majestic. In his presence I felt intelligent. Attractive. And unique. Always available for my impromptu visits, he never gave me the awkward impression of being disturbed.

A great lover of the Apocrypha literature, as my father would later be. He had taught it intermittently for starvation wages at the Institute for Jewish Studies. He supported his family by working in a modest publishing house that put out an encyclopedia of biographies and Judaic quotations. He also gave private courses in Yiddish and Hebrew to candidates for conversion. Oddly enough, he bought lottery tickets every month. "I'm not a fatalist as was Ibn Ezra in Spain," he used to say. "He was so convinced that he would remain poor all his life that he thought if he were a candle salesman the sun would never set; if he were an undertaker no one would ever die." That's why he bought lottery tickets—to prove his theory. He was also a gambler. Did he sometimes win? The fact is my grandmother never complained of being out of pocket.

Was he religious? Devout? Yes and no. Let's say he was a traditionalist. Out of respect for his parents, his ancestors, particularly Rabbi Petahia, he observed the Sabbath, put on phylacteries in the morning, and studied the Talmud, not because he saw it as a holy and immutable document, but because he found correspondences and points of reference in it that related to his curiosity about some officially marginalized or concealed book that didn't have the good fortune of being included in the canon.

My mother, when she's not in the company of others, is timid, overly prudent, anxious. She often sits motionless with a book on her knees, barely swings her hips when she moves about. The daughter of parents born in New York, she wasn't traumatized by the war. A homemaker, she kept house and dreamed of having grandchildren. Itzhak was barely thirteen and she already teased him: "So, son, when will you be getting married?" She left me in peace. Actually, I think she wanted to keep us by her side, my brother and me, for as long as possible.

As for the theater, it was my grandfather who mentioned it to me, perhaps unwittingly.

He had been my confidant since childhood. At ten, I used to tell him about my dreams, my doubts, my disappointments. Sometimes he asked me what I wanted to be when I grew up. My answers were never the same. One day it was gardener, the next day sailor, mathematician, parachutist, silversmith, musician, painter, banker, snake charmer: the list was inexhaustible. Then, smiling in his beard, my grandfather would say, "You really want to be all these things?"

"Yes," I replied, naively. "Is it impossible?"

"No. For a child your age, everything should seem possible."

"Everything? At the same time?"

"At the same time, if . . ."

"If what?"

"If you accept a profession that includes them all."

"What could that be?"

"Writer. Novelist."

"What's that?"

"Someone who writes. Someone whose life is writing. Then, man is a book: all the stories can be contained inside. It's a world that exists in your head, inhabited by all men. Words that make one sing."

"Do you want him to write fiction?"

"Why not?"

"And what if that man doesn't write?" asked the little boy.

"If it isn't his vocation? Then he talks."

"And he can still do as many things?"

"Yes. And many more."

"How?"

"There's the stage," he said—he of all people, for he had never set foot in a theater and yet knew it thoroughly.

The word had been uttered, and it carried me into the faraway landscape of illusions, lived and shared.

However, when I embarked on my studies in the dramatic arts and told him of my anxieties and joys as I learned to perform Aeschylus and Pirandello, Racine and Tennessee Williams, he constantly warned me not to entertain extravagant hopes, even in this area. As for me, the only thing I thought about was the emotion you feel onstage.

"Grandfather, it's an experience that summons all the senses of the body and engages it completely: you look at a performance, you listen to it, you absorb it. Painting, sculpture, music, and movement merge in front of your eyes. Imagine, every night on a platform as narrow as a garret, the actors partake in the creation of a world with its passions, ambitions, sorrows, and moments of enlightenment."

"And afterward, when the performance is over, what do they do?" my grandfather retorted. "Where do they go? To the restaurant? The bar? And they repeat the same thing, exactly the same thing, the following day?"

"That's exactly it, Grandfather. That's the miraculous side of theater. Repetition itself becomes creation."

He took his time thinking it over. Had my argument convinced him? Did he consider himself defeated? He changed his strategy and gave me advice that turned out to be valuable to me in the future.

"Still, don't forget, son, theater is just theater and nothing more. An illusion lived in the present. Once the doors close, another life takes up where you left it, another truth, more enduring perhaps, indeed irrevocable; in the end, the actor who dies onstage will not get back up again."

"Will I have to choose between the two lives, Grandfather?"

"No, my child. You have to integrate one into the other. The actor who pretends to be weeping today will burst out laughing tomorrow. Just as the philosopher's truth is tested and created in doubt, the actor finds his truth in metamorphosis. You're surprised I'm using these words? You shouldn't be. I like to read and I like words. I watch some words get old and others die young. They, too, are in theater, in their own way."

He also used to say to me: "Furthermore, don't forget that in our tradition the book is more important than the stage. It teaches us that God is King as well as Judge: man is His subject, His servant, His tool, and His cornerstone, but not His plaything. For the Jew, living in His collective memory, the world is not a spectacle. I knew a time when cruel individuals usurped the power of God and perverted it with unfeigned cruelty."

As I said, my grandfather had known the camps. Grandmother, too, somewhere in Hungary. They never spoke about it. When people referred to them, Grandmother would turn pale and set her lips. They had met on a refugee boat on the way to America.

For me, a little Jewish-American boy, disoriented and awkward, Hungary and Romania, Poland and Austria belonged to a distant, obscure mythology.

In spite of my timidity and bouts of sadness, which worried my parents, I was a happy child. I liked eating my meals with them, did my homework with care, laughed when I heard a funny story—in short, my life felt comfortable.

With hindsight, I realize that as far as my vocation was concerned, my mother wasn't completely wrong. A few years in law school would have helped me in my work as a journalist. Particularly when I was covering the trial that would have an impact on my destiny, though not as much as on young Werner Sonderberg's, Hans Dunkelman's nephew on the paternal side. I know, you're puzzled by the different names. Why did the nephew decide to change his last name? You might even find the answer upsetting. Be patient. We'll get to that when the time comes.

Itzhak made my mother happy early on: no sooner had he graduated from university than he married a fellow student, Orli, the most beautiful young woman in his class. She was cheerful, had a kindly face, a shapely body. Her father, a Wall Street stockbroker and a very Orthodox Jew, laid down two conditions before consenting to their union: that the marriage be celebrated in the Hasidic tradition and that his son-in-law work with him.

On the day of the wedding, hundreds of guests assembled in the reception rooms of a large hotel. Three rabbis officiated at the ceremony. Dozens of students from the yeshiva subsidized by the family sang and danced in honor of the young couple. Just seeing the fiancé and his beloved carried on the shoulders of the dancers to the sound of two orchestras filled me with joy, though it became tinged with a vague melancholy when I noticed my grandfather weeping under the huppah: I felt a pang of anguish without understanding why. My grandmother was weeping, too, but tearlessly. I heard her whisper into my grandfather's ear, "Do you think they see us?" Whom did she mean by "they"? The members of the family who had remained in Europe. Lost in the turmoil.

Itzhak and Orli had four children, two girls and two boys.

On a holiday evening, when the whole family was assembled around the table, I heard my mother whisper to my father, "Look, in spite of it all, we've defeated Hitler. Our happiness is his hell."

And then again, I saw tears well up in my grandfather's eyes, he who was so good at hiding his feelings. He seemed absent, very far away, lost in the past, no doubt.

He had told us that Rabbi Petahia was born in the Carpathian Mountains, near the village where the great Rabbi

Israel Baal Shem Tov used to take solitary walks dreaming of the mysteries of Creation. Unusual powers were attributed to him: by subtly combining the letters in some mystical prayers and in the names of the angels by the side of the Creator, it was said he could change the fate of individuals.

One day, when he was still in his youth, Rabbi Petahia was approached by a woman in tears. She had been wandering on the road for two days and two nights looking for help. Her husband was sick; he was going to die. She would be left with their six little children. They were hungry. No one in the world was prepared to help her. "Have pity on us," the woman lamented. "Save my children. You, Rabbi, who arrange so many things, arrange for my husband to stay alive." And Rabbi Petahia, moved to tears, could not ignore her request. But he had been warned about the heavens: man is not allowed to change the laws of nature, laws created and willed by God. Rabbi Petahia did not listen to the heavenly voice. "I'm prepared to accept my punishment, provided the sick man is not summoned to the world of truth and can remain with his family. I'm aware that the miracle will be done at my expense, and I say: Amen, so be it." And he said to the woman, "Go home, your husband has his children by his side; they are joyfully awaiting you." Of course he was deprived of his powers. For a month. And to mankind's misfortune, he made the decision that from then on he would never again rebel against God's will.

Several months later, he got married.

AS FOR ME, I waited a long time before getting married. Out of fear of life, of not being able to support a family? Yet I hoped to have a close relationship with a beautiful and intelligent woman. And Alika possessed these attributes, or virtues. But, for reasons that escaped me, I wasn't ready.

It was she who insisted that I put an end to my bachelorhood. After three years of living together, she decreed that it was time for her to become, as she put it, "an honest woman."

We met at the university, where we were both studying drama. No other area attracted me. The sciences? Inconceivable. Mathematics had always been a terrifying mystery for me. Theology? My relations with God left a lot to be desired. But why not geography, economics, anthropology, architecture, or psychology? Why theater? Was it because it occupies a minor, virtually nonexistent, position in the Jewish tradition? Yet the tradition offered thousands of examples of eloquence. Jeremiah, Isaiah, Amos: these prophets' words were fiery and impassioned. Rabbi Akiba, Rabbi

Ishmael, Rabbi Yohanan ben Zakkai: masters of language. Rashi and his commentaries, Maimonides and his philosophy, Nahmanides and his disputations with the convert Pablo Christiani. The Gaon Elijah of Vilnius: "The goal of redemption is the Redemption of the Truth." Interpreters, visionaries, precursors. All erudite men in search of meaning. Still, for them, the world was not a stage, nor was life a performance. Was their universe too serious? Lacking in humor and fantasy? Incapable of arousing laughter and nurturing the imagination?

Perhaps I simply wanted to take my grandfather's advice. I often used to recall the conversation we had had. Was life a string of roles? A series of rough drafts? A kaleidoscope? As for my professor at the university, he believed in theater. He made us read, read, and read—in this he was like my grandfather—whatever came into his head. Aristotle's rules on drama, Nietzsche's *Birth of Tragedy,* Euripides, Ionesco, the Bible, and the Vedas. Psychology and theological treatises, Strindberg, Anski, Goethe, Pirandello, Shaw, Beckett: I devoured them and they devoured me. We had to study the methods of Stanislavski, Vakhtangov, Jouvet, and the Actors Studio. He admired Meyerhold not for his theories but for his ultimate fate: shot in 1940 on personal orders from Stalin. Attentive to every word, watching every movement of the arms and lips. I never stopped wondering: How can the enactment of representation be changed into living truth? How does the actor manage to make a thousand spectators believe, for two hours, that he is another person? He recites borrowed words and appropriates them as though they originated in his own brain and heart, and they move me as if they were just being formulated in my presence. This miracle of metamorphosis inherent to art, I was living it intensely enough to devote my dreams to it, my ambitions, my escapes, my needs—in short: my youthful years.

One day, the professor surprised us by citing Augustine: "God is close to those who flee from him, and flees from those who seek him." And he added the following comment: "In a way this is true of the actor, too. I am close and far at the same time. My body can be touched, but I remain mentally inaccessible: the spectator sees me, but he can't enter my thoughts. The body is present and so is the soul, in a different way. To perform is a bit like making the invisible visible, but only for an instant. That's the grandeur and trap for the actor. If I want to be too detached, I will be bad; if I overidentify with the character, I will be bad, too. On the stage, self-effacement is sometimes necessary in order to acquire another self. But more often, the two selves quarrel, make peace, share their daily bread; and that becomes a work of art." To paraphrase Jean-Paul Sartre: in a play you must lie to be true.

From the first day, Alika and I formed not a couple but a duo. It was our professor—a short, bearded man with a quavering, mischievous voice, a face furrowed in perpetual astonishment and, perhaps, a skeptic's self-mockery—who had wished it. Without knowing our names yet, just our faces, he had pointed to the two of us: "You and you, you're going to read page twelve of the play." For a while afterward, I jokingly called her "you" and she called me "you."

Oh, the good-hearted professor with the bushy beard and inquisitive gaze. His every word counted. His influence weighed on my every step, and on my decisions, too.

I remember our first sessions. Fervor, a feverish desire to learn, intense excitement: simple words became rich and sacred; innocuous gestures took on a meaning that sublimated them. Every day brought a revelation about human nature, its ugliness, and made us discover the whims of fate and of men.

"Theater is not a profession," said our professor with a solemn and grave air. "Remember: it's a vocation, a mission. An *initiation.* Better yet: a form of asceticism. When you're playing Othello, or you, Phaedra, you're not operetta heroes but princes, gods; you expect the spectators to bow before you in order to receive from your lips, if not from your hands, not the punishment of the earth but a fiery offering."

With his calm and firm voice, he emphasized that we should each take account of our own morphology and determine how to extract from it the essence of words and the magic of gestures. But above all he was a spiritual guide; what he tried to fashion was our souls. He taught us how to read in depth, how to assimilate a text and savor it before making it into sheer song, the song transmitted to us by generations of guides and students.

In one of our first classes, with a facetious look on his face, he kept us standing and silent for an hour in order to teach us how to emphasize presence in absence and movement in motionlessness.

"Fear," he remarked. "How can fear be incarnated? By trembling? No. By laughing and dancing a certain way. I'd almost be tempted to say by experiencing a great joy. A hidden but all-consuming fear, repressed but enveloping: that's what you show the audience. Everything within you is afraid: your thought processes are afraid of being too slow or too quick, too visible or not visible enough; your soul is afraid of wanting to be too free or not really a prisoner. At that moment, onstage, you are fear itself."

On another occasion: "Onstage, you must know how to laugh and cry as if for the first time. Think about Nietzsche's madness celebrating the virtue of laughter. And of Dante, who pities the damned in the ninth circle because they can't weep. And above all, think of Virgil, who says fortunate is the person who can understand the secret causes of things. From all three, the actor has much to learn."

And on another occasion: "In his rigor as much as in his vulnerability, the actor develops in his temporary role a role that defies and overwhelms him before it liberates him. Admittedly, he knows his part from the start, just as he knows his partner's lines, nothing is improvised, and yet his words and movements must not *seem* spontaneous but *be* spontaneous."

Fascinated, the students were riveted to everything he said.

He continued in his deep voice tinged with ironic melancholy: "You won't be surprised to hear me say that for human beings life is often a game: whether princes or beggars, rich or poor, erudite or ignorant, they all have one thing in common: they more or less feign sincerity. And among them, of course, I like the actor best. He will be alone when the day comes that he will have to leave the stage. In politics as in business, nothing is more distressing than the sight of an old man refusing to give up the privileges of his position. For the actor, it isn't the same: even when he is old, he will have a part to play, the part of the old man. But whether young or not, the art of leaving the stage, when the time comes, is the hardest one to acquire; arriving is simple, leaving is not. You'll learn that here."

Alika whispers to me in an aside: "You got that, right? If one of us decides to break up, he will have to do so with artful delicacy."

Born in California, an only daughter, Alika came from a well-to-do, liberal family, secular if not atheist. She had her first real Sabbath meal in our house at my mother's invitation. And she only began to fast on Yom Kippur to please me. We saw a great deal of each other for weeks on end, in our courses and for occasional rehearsals in her studio apartment in Greenwich Village, or in mine, which wasn't very far from hers. It was a comfortable camaraderie, with ordinary meetings between friends, a relationship with no physical contact. In fact, she had warned me quite frankly: "I've known men before you, both older and younger, so please don't fall in love; it could ruin our relationship." I promised her. It was easy, particularly since I was recovering from an unhappy love affair and I wasn't ready to embark on a new romance.

Today, I think about it with amusement: our professor thought it useful and necessary to teach us how to make people laugh and how to make them dream—making them dream was more complicated because it was more subtle. How to look on in silence and make this silence be part of the spectacle. How to embrace one another and even how to kiss. Our first kiss was directed; it had no spontaneity. I don't recall whether I enjoyed it. But I acquired a taste for it. Later on.

And, one evening, it happened.

It happened thanks to Alika's cousin, Sharon. She was working on a film in Hollywood and had come to New York for a few days. The three of us dined together in the Village, in a small restaurant popular with students. We had a long discussion about the latest best-selling novel adapted to the screen. Alika was against it on principle, Sharon for. I was against it, too, but I supported her cousin's point of view. I liked her spirit and enthusiasm. At the end of the stormy meal, the young woman said she was tired and wanted to return to her hotel.

As it was on my way, I offered to walk her back. Alika objected. We had course work to do for the next day—on the subject, as I recall, of the blind man in drama and the modern transposition of his nightmares. Script in hand, we worked on our parts. Suddenly she stopped and stared at me for a long time. Was she jealous? In any case, her agitation added to her charm. But to this day I have no idea whether she suddenly found me attractive or was afraid of my leaving her.

The rest, as they say, was an event staged in heaven.

The Talmud says that having completed the job of creation, God, suddenly unemployed, set to work arranging marriages. Sometimes, though not always, it's love at first sight. At other times, the process can last years. Yedidyah wonders about the heavenly marriage broker's method: What are his criteria in making his choices? And what about divorces—who is responsible for divorces?

And what about the crimes of men?

Did Hans, Werner's uncle, believe in God? Did Werner? At the trial he was asked many questions, but not that one. It's a shame.

My annual medical exam. Dr. Feldman doesn't utter a word from beginning to end. He lets the body express itself in its own way. Its language is more familiar to him. He receives its signals with his hands. If he smiles, that's good. If he remains impassive, it's because something is troubling him.

Today he isn't smiling.

He wants to know if I sleep well; no, I sleep badly. I always have. Do I exercise every morning? No. Never. I don't have the time or the patience.

"Well, all of this is going to change," he says. "I'm prescribing a diet for you. It's in your best interest to follow it."

I tell him that I don't feel sick, but that if he insists, I could play the part of Molière's "imaginary invalid."

"That's not funny," he says.

Yedidyah and his uncle Méir were very close. As a child, he liked to play chess with him, get his advice, listen to his stories of fallen angels and laughing demons.

Méir and his brother had escaped the horrors of the great turmoil. Yedidyah's grandfather, in his premonitory wisdom, had sent them to a distant relative in Brooklyn, supposedly as yeshiva students. He said, "Before facing Esau, his brother and enemy, Patriarch Jacob separated his relatives into two camps. So if one were to die, the other would survive. Just in case." Clearly he was right. But did the two brothers feel guilty for having "abandoned" or "betrayed" their parents in obeying them? If so, they never showed it.

Méir was madly in love with his wife. In fact, she called him "my big lunatic" in the morning and "my little lunatic" at night. Hence the nickname the family gave him: "Méir the little lunatic." It was claimed that whenever he wanted to he could blind himself to reality in order to better discover invisible worlds: his blindness and his clairvoyance went hand in hand. But he wasn't at all mad. Or blind. Little Yedidyah had a thousand and one proofs of this.

Admittedly, he had a fertile, passionate imagination: he saw some things more clearly and more farsightedly than anyone else. But is that madness? Couldn't it be regarded instead as a power that Wise Men pride themselves on having? Occasionally he abolished time; past and future were equally important to him and he slid from one to the other with disconcerting ease. This was because he liked to catch people off guard.

One day, as Méir and Yedidyah were strolling down the street—sometimes he would pick up his nephew at school—he pointed to a hurried passerby.

"Take a good look, my child," he said. "He has no idea where he's going, but he's running. Whereas I know where he's going. One look at his face and I know everything about his life. Do you want me to tell you? His wife doesn't love him; he keeps suspecting she's unfaithful to him. He has two children who fight over every little thing. A neighbor who hates him. He's plagued with insomnia. He's had a great tragedy in his life: his first child, a daughter, was born handicapped. Ever since, he's been cursing himself day and night."

"Can we help him?"

"Yes. You could."

"How?"

"You could sing a song for him. Go on, run, catch up with him. You'll change the star controlling his life."

Yedidyah looked around for the passerby. Too late. He had disappeared. And Méir noted, "That's the misfortune. We never do things in time."

The words of a lunatic? No, those of a wise man.

Another day, Méir noticed an old woman in tears. "She's lost her handbag. It contains all her papers. And all her remaining money: she'd just withdrawn it from the bank. But don't worry. I'll help her. She'll get everything back. And she'll laugh. And then cry. Out of happiness."

"How will you do it?"

"We'll do it together."

And the amazing thing was, an hour later, Yedidyah saw the old lady again.

She was laughing.

Yedidyah finally asked the question bluntly: "Tell me, Méir. They say you became blind, but I know you're not. They also say you're mad. Is it true?"

"It is, my child. I'm mad, a blind lunatic, blinded by madness, blinded by the thick, dark light that envelops this world where we're condemned to live. And this light affects my reason to the point of diverting it, perturbing it, directing it against itself, against its source. Do you understand what I just said?"

"No, Meir. I don't."

"Very good. Bravo. You could have lied. To please me. You chose to tell the truth. Beware—one day, you, too, might be called a lunatic."

With the years, he stopped being interested in newspapers. He didn't even ask Drora or Yedidyah—when he came to visit—to read the papers to him. He used to say: "What's the point? I know what's in them. The situations and events are always the same; the names alone change. Therefore we might as well leaf through the phone book, right?"

He recounted how he had met Drora. In a museum in Paris. They were admiring the same Rembrandt painting: Abraham being stopped from sacrificing Isaac. She was oriental, simultaneously stern and dreamy. They left together and, without a word, sat down at the terrace of a café. She asked him to tell her a story. He invented more than one; but he spoke differently to Yedidyah.

"It was during the Occupation, a boy and a girl. Courageous. Their mission: to follow a traitor and track down where he lived. They saw him go home one night, a summer night. They went back to her house. They made love and were happy for a very long time: for a whole night. A small fragment of eternity. For others, eternity is what comes after death; for lovers, it's what precedes it."

"Who was it? Drora?"

He smiled but didn't answer.

Yedidyah loved him.

And he loved being loved.

As for me, I love children. And of course, my twins are the children I love most in the world. Intelligent, respectful of others, they embody the joy of ever-renewed surprises. I need only look at them or listen to them and I thank God for having invented life and happiness and the family. Thanks to them, more than once, Alika and I grew close after a quarrel, big or small.

Leibele and Dovid'l: the same delicate face, the same dark eyes, the same penetrating and peaceful gaze, the same husky voice. And, give or take a few tiny differences, the same character and the same fondness for medieval music. They've always been very close even if each one had his own temperament. Leibele, being pragmatic, studied architecture, whereas Dovid'l chose philosophy of science. The former always sought the company of people, while the latter shied away from them, taking refuge inside his books.

Misfortune struck when they both fell in love with the same woman, a beautiful brunette full of talent, humor, and surprises. When she shared our meals, the dining room radiated with warmth and wit. What happened next? It was to be expected: each spared the other's feelings; the two brothers broke up with her at the same time. Together they succeeded in overcoming feelings of guilt, but Dovid'l left for Israel to complete his studies. He was wounded in a bomb attack. Leibele departed immediately to be at his bedside. A few weeks later, Dovid'l sent us a reassuring letter from the Tel Hashomer hospital:

My dear parents,

I know you're worried about me. I can understand—I would be worried, too, if I were in your position, but I'm getting better. I'm being taken care of by marvelous physicians. The nurses are gentle and beautiful. When Eve smiles at me, I don't feel the pain of the injection. I'm almost tempted to request a second one. If this continues, I'll fall in love with her.

My accident? Leibele must have told you everything. I was strolling in the narrow streets of Jerusalem, near the main market. I like the brouhaha and the odors. The crush of people. The kids running from one stall to another, trying to filch a candy or a fruit while the merchants find it amusing and let them get away with it. The Talmudists going over the morning class. The housewives with their shopping bags. The place is teeming with people; everyone is bustling about. Here life is simple.

And suddenly everything disappeared in the explosion. All I remember is I fell. I woke up in the hospital. What had happened? A terrorist had just accomplished his suicide mission. Five dead. Sixteen wounded. Including me. Shrapnel in my stomach and in my right leg. Operation successful. A few weeks in the hospital. Everything will be okay. Later.

As usual, the attack aroused anger and frustration throughout the country. How is it possible to justify the cult of death so many young Palestinians adhere to? Forensic scientists, working on the autopsy of the terrorist, found that he was smiling as he set off the destructive device. His face reflected neither hatred nor terror but a kind of anticipation; he welcomed death, his and his victims', with a smile.

I don't understand.

Leibele, who comes to see me every day, thinks the man was brainwashed and believed in the legend of the seventy virgins promised in heaven by the Koran. Fanaticism? Let's not pass judgment on religion, though we're allowed to condemn people who pervert it for political ends.

I was told that two hours after the explosion, the market was back to its normal activity. The pupils in the neighboring schools were already quietly sitting and listening to their teachers.

The market . . . I'm eager to return to it. With a bit of luck, I'll manage to persuade Eve to come with me.

Your Dovid'l who loves you

P.S. Mom, a suggestion: someone should make a film about these young assassins who think they're making God happy by killing His children. And you, Dad: How about coming to Jerusalem and doing a story for your paper?

Yedidyah was considering going to join the twins, whom he missed more than anything in the world, when Leibele informed his parents that he was dropping out of university and enlisting in the Israeli army. He quickly became a member of a commando, filling his parents with a mixture of pride and fear.

Some time later, a Hebrew newspaper ran an article in his praise. The title: "Honor to Leibele! Bravo!" He was commanding an operation in Gaza; the aim was to capture a terrorist leader responsible for several attacks in Tel Aviv and bring him back alive. A spectacular success. With no loss of human life.

"You see?" Yedidyah said to Alika. "Theater isn't the only thing to live for."

"You're right," she answered. "The papers allude to the 'theater of operations,' but war isn't theater. On that particular stage, the dead don't get back up."

Yedidyah made a gesture of discouragement. "Unfortunately, among those who declare war, there are surely some, here as elsewhere, for whom it's a game staged by believers far away who claim to be acting in the name of their God."

One of his son's comments filled him with emotion and convinced him to make the trip to Israel: "Let it not be said," Leibele had recently written, "that the descendant of the great Rabbi Petahia failed to join his people when they were in danger."

And Yedidyah said to himself that, clearly, history was not a game.

And yet. He wondered how so much suffering could be

explained in this world, a world hidden under the mask of hatred, like a shroud, as a way of extinguishing the last sparks of sensibility and hope from it. How is one to act so this suffering would successfully transcend history by humanizing it?

Recalling the past, his grandfather had said to him one day, "You often hear people say, regarding some event, history will be the judge. Actually, history itself will be judged."

"In other words," Yedidyah noted, "Creation may be just one big, lengthy court proceeding?"

"Yes, you might say that."

"And where does God fit in, Grandfather?" Yedidyah asked.

His grandfather didn't answer.

Each time Yedidyah hears the word "trial," inevitably Kafka's trial is the one that comes to his mind: "Someone must have been telling lies about Josef K."

Lies, many lies, were told about the young German Werner Sonderberg. How had he managed to cope? As he faced the huge, all-powerful judicial apparatus, he had remained impassive, as if immunized in his isolation. Yedidyah described the young man, but he didn't really understand him. Many events had filled his memory since then, from both the general situation and his private life, but the trial had receded in his mind without fading away. Had his approach to things changed, his trajectory? Had the defendant's behavior made him sense something that might have influenced his conception of justice, if not of good and evil? If he had changed, at what precise moment? And what part had Alika played in all of this? Had he grown closer to her, or drifted away from her?

There was one incident that could have turned into a disaster.

Alika was playing in Chekhov's *The Three Sisters.*

"Do me a favor," she said to Yedidyah. "Don't come to see the play."

Afraid he would be ashamed of her? He had gone nevertheless. Secretly. With a pang of anguish, he had waited in the dark for the curtain to rise and had slipped into the silent theater. He took a seat in the next-to-last row. Alika lives for the theater; her dream is to go onstage. Will she live up to the challenge? Will she thrill the audience, tense in its quest for beauty and truth, for the old to become new, alternating between the known and unknown? Will she act well? And if not, how could he tell her without wounding her and endangering their love? She acted well, in fact very well. But it was not the right part. Instead of playing the part of Masha, the unfortunate, unhappy wife, she had chosen the part of the youngest sister, Irina, who was nervous, restless, and scatterbrained. Alika was not very good at incarnating a character that did not suit her.

Would she find out that he had disobeyed? The subject never came up.

Dr. Feldman and I see each other often. This morning he makes me open my mouth and examines my tongue.

"I don't like it," he says.

"I'm sorry, Doctor, but it's the only one I have."

He doesn't appreciate my humor.

Actually, the good doctor doesn't like anything about me. And even less my heart. He doesn't like the way I'm breathing. He thinks I tire too quickly. He wants to know whether, by any chance, my parents had heart conditions. No, not as far as I know. Perhaps someone else in my family? No one.

"Still, you ought to be careful," the doctor says insistently.

It is imperative, he says, that I treat my body as a friend. Otherwise, it might become my enemy. And then it would be a nuisance for my physician, and even more so for me.

ISRAEL: I DIDN'T EXPECT such emotion to arise in me from being there. I saw my two sons again and wept: my heart overflowed with pride. We spent a week together. I thanked heaven for each hour, each sigh, and each gaze. Suddenly turning sentimental, I catch myself using religious terms. What the Besht and the Gaon of Vilnius, Rabbis Berdichev and Wischnitz, in exile, could see only in their dreams, I am enjoying in reality.

Jerusalem: as I climbed up its hills, monuments of green vegetation soaring up to a blue sky, my heart began to race and I almost forgot to breathe. This is what my distant ancestors must have felt when they made their pilgrimage to the Temple three times a year. In the Talmud it says that the pilgrims could number one million, yet no one complained of lack of space or discomfort. My grandfather believed this. Were there any journalists in those days?

This trip still leaves its stamp. As incomparable as the city of David itself. Wherever I walk, said Rabbi Nahman of Bratslav, each step brings me closer to Jerusalem, the city that, more than any other, embodies what is eternal in the memory of my people.

After the Sonderberg trial and its unexpected outcome, Paul, my boss and friend, appointed me, at my request and for a very brief period, special correspondent in Israel. You need a change of scenery? The choice was Europe or Israel. Just as in the past when it came to theater and journalism, it was my grandfather who suggested the Holy City.

"Go there as my ambassador," he urged me. "As my personal family representative. Remember carefully: like my father and his father, I live with the feeling of having lived in Jerusalem; I'm eager to return there with you, through you; I've prayed in front of the Wall, and I'd like to see it again through your eyes. Through you, I'll reimmerse myself in my memories. Don't forget: my memory and yours must blend into his."

In fact, he had been there only once. At a time when he was still in mourning for the death of my grandmother. Disconsolate, inconsolable, he spent his days studying and his nights praying. A forty-eight-hour lightning-quick visit. Officially he was supposed to see an old companion who was ill. But his real objective was more sentimental: to stroll around the Old City of Jerusalem. Recite the Psalms there. Find an elusive nostalgia. Hear reverberations of the prophets' tragic warnings. Commune in front of the Wall and think about our ancestor, the illustrious Cabbalist, Rabbi Petahia, whose interpretation of the Names fires the imagination. Why didn't he stay there? Was he unwilling to part from us? Was he afraid of starting a new life? No. I think I heard him murmur that regardless of where he's from, a Jew feels at home on the soil of the prophets. That, for a Jew, living in Israel is a privilege: the privilege of coming home again. And that this privilege he didn't deserve.

But he came home a changed man.

"That whole story concerning the young German that you're obsessed with, over there, you'll understand it better, and more deeply," he said to me one day. "So many enemies have tried to destroy our people; the most recent one, in Germany, almost succeeded. Could all civilizations be mortal? You might think so. But there is Jerusalem."

"According to the wise Rabbi Shaul," my grandfather said, "the God of Israel did not invest four thousand years of faith and defiance in the history of his people in order to one day see them annihilated. And yet, at the time of the great Tragedy, the enemy had almost succeeded at it. Far from Jerusalem, it had almost destroyed Jerusalem. You've read the book of Ezekiel, haven't you? He describes his vision of dry bones in the desert. And he predicts that one day they will come back to life. And yet, son, for the first time in our history, the dead had no right to a grave. The enemy even eliminated their bones, threw their ashes in the rivers, or scattered them in the wind. Think of that in

Jerusalem when you dream of my Jerusalem. You won't forget?"

"No, Grandfather. I won't forget."

As fate would have it, on the day I arrived trouble flared up on the southern border. An Israeli soldier was killed and three others wounded. Widespread turmoil and a wave of anger swept over the country. An infernal cycle that had become routine. Attack and counterattack. Aggression and reprisals. Kill the killers. And invariably, blood flows. And some children become orphans. And where does peace fit in? And the suffering of the stranger, known and unknown? Invariably, it is Death that comes out victorious. I visit the southern and central borders. I ask questions and listen. Rabbis and pupils, soldiers and civilians. Young vagabonds and old beggars. Political personalities and writers. How much longer will this era of uncertainty last? How can hatred be stopped? But how can terrorism be defeated if not through counterterrorism, that is, by spurning the glorious principle according to which every human life is sacred? How can we act so that the tears of joy of one don't cause the anguished sobs of another? So that the hope of one isn't based on the despair of another?

An oriental rabbi, with a fiery gaze and an impassioned expression, demands that his entire generation exercise vigilance as it waits for redemption.

An eloquent novelist pleads for the universalization of

the Jewish ethic: improve the human condition of the Palestinians in the Territories; recognize their abiding right to self-determination.

For a left-wing politician, there is no other solution but the creation of two independent sovereign states living side by side in security and peace.

His right-wing opponent sees this plan as utopian. The terrorist in the enemy camp doesn't want territorial concessions; his dream is the creation of a single state. A Palestinian state. Built on our corpses.

A human rights activist blames me for not helping the Palestinian cause. I reply: "Let them stop the terrorist violence and there will be many of us embracing it."

I dedicate my story to my grandfather. I address him. It is to him that I relate my discoveries, the things that make me proud, those that frighten me, those that rend my heart.

Suddenly I think of the great Nikolai Gogol: on returning from Jerusalem, he burned part two of his book *Dead Souls.* I can understand him: the experience of Jerusalem is too powerful, too intense. Faced with it, words inevitably lose their vigor. Purifying them by fire then becomes a possibility, as shown by Rabbi Nahman of Bratslav and Franz Kafka.

Let me explain.

A beautiful, aristocratic woman with a haughty bearing. Around forty. Her only son, a Tzahal lieutenant, was killed when he threw himself on a grenade to protect his comrades. She visits his grave every morning. She tells him about the events of the day. I ask her if she thinks she will ever know happiness again, in the near or distant future. She looks at me in silence. As though she had understood not the meaning of my question but the very nature of my Jewishness.

I feel like talking to her about my sons, but I'm afraid she will break down in tears. About Alika then? About my love for her, or my attachment to my grandfather? In spite of his past, so fraught with grief and bereavement, he remains open to joy, a joy so different from mine or the joy of most men: it seems drawn from a source known to him alone. But I am aware that this sort of comparison is displaced. Two instances of grief add up without canceling each other. One doesn't justify the other, even if it explains it. Incapable of consoling her, I feel at loose ends, disoriented, useless. Should I kiss her on the cheek? I choose to do nothing and say nothing. May my respectful and wounded silence be an offering.

Let me explain.

My last hours in Jerusalem, in the Old City. I spend a sleepless night thinking things through.

I had promised my grandfather that I wouldn't forget the past, the past that haunted him. How was I to reconcile Auschwitz and Jerusalem? Would the former merely be the antithesis, the anti-event of the latter? If Auschwitz is forever the question, is Jerusalem forever the answer? On the one hand the darkness of the abyss, on the other the dazzling light of daybreak? At Birkenau and Treblinka, the burning bush was consumed, but here the flame continues to warm the hearts of messianic dreamers.

What is the meaning of all this?

Let me explain.

I catch myself having a sudden desire to pray. I pray for Alika: may she find serenity. For my two children: may they find fulfillment in a world rid of all cruelty, cynicism, and pain, and all forms of fanaticism. For my uncle Méir: may his madness continue to bring beauty and not intellectual decline. For my grandfather: may he still live a long time, may he find the strength to recount what can only be expressed by song or silence.

Let me explain.

The beggars, whose palms and mouths were constantly open, even when there wasn't a single tourist in sight. Not one answered my questions, but they all made me offerings that have greater weight than the best of replies. I collect their stories with a deep sense of gratitude.

The story of the two drops of water in the ocean that look for each other in vain and meet only when solitude and nostalgia turn them into tears—I got this story from one of them. I regard it as a treasure that it is incumbent upon me to safeguard.

I say to him: it could be that God set me on man's earth for the express purpose of this meeting here tonight, in the shadow of the shades that roam before the Wall, and to listen to you.

Suddenly, facing the remains of the ancient Temple,

where countless pilgrims have come to express their thirst for truth and redemption, I realize that, for the first time in a long time, far from Alika, I haven't lived or even approached experience in theatrical terms.

Perhaps because here neither fate nor history appears as a spectacle that can be interrupted or canceled at will.

Like my grandfather, when I returned to New York I was no longer the same.

AND JOURNALISM? AND THE TRIAL? Werner and Anna. The young German would like to see me. What does he want to talk to me about? Does he want to compare notes, the notes of the actor with the notes of the spectator?

So I was a journalist. I began my career as a drama critic. Yet it had never occurred to me; it had never been one of my ambitions. Actually, I owe being cast in this part to our bearded professor with the mischievous expression.

During my third year of study, he gave me to understand—and hardly with kid gloves—that he couldn't see me leading a useful or honorable life on the stage.

"You like the theater, that's for sure," he said to me one day. "It means a lot to you, that's obvious, and I like that. But I can't see you on the boards."

And after a pause for dramatic effect: "I see you in the audience."

Some of my classmates started to laugh while I felt crushed. Alika lost her temper. "You morons, you find this funny? Professor, how can you enjoy humiliating a student in public?"

He hastened to correct himself. "Pay no attention to the wiseguys, my son. You're superior to them. In fact, you're the best in the class. But . . ."

"But what?" Alika asked insistently. "Go on. Don't stop in the middle of a nasty remark."

He didn't answer her, but invited me to come and see him after class in his office.

I expected criticism, or worse: a condescending lesson to make me understand, for once and for all, that I was a hopeless actor. And I wasn't completely mistaken.

We were standing in front of the window giving out on a garden. He put his hand on my shoulder and said, "Listen to me carefully, my son. I'm convinced of what I said, though I was wrong to say it in the middle of class in front of everyone, and I hope you'll forgive me. I'd like you to understand something very simple: there's more than one way of being crazy about theater. It's a love that can be expressed through writing, directing, acting, music, lighting design, and even—after all, we're talking about gifts in the literal sense of the word—by financing shows. Yes, don't look at me like that. Theater is a passion and also an art, and isn't art the most sublime form of generosity?"

"In other words, Professor, your advice to me is to earn a lot of money first, is that it? To become a rich donor, the sponsor of a theater company, and to live my whole life as an onlooker?"

"No," the professor replied, looking solemn. "That's not my advice to you."

"Then . . ."

"My advice to you is to never stray from the theater. It's your world, your universe; I'm even tempted to say your salvation. It will justify your life and give it meaning."

"But how am I to achieve this?"

He paused for a long time before replying, "I'll give it some thought. When I come up with the answer, I'll let you know."

A few weeks later, he summoned me to his office again. On that day, he sat at his desk as he welcomed me in.

"You'll become a drama critic."

"But I'm not qualified! I've never written a thing. I'll never be able to! I'm not a journalist!"

"You're knowledgeable about theater, you love it, you live and breathe theater with all your heart and intellect. That's all that matters."

And that's how, to Alika's astonishment and the joy of all my relatives, including my grandfather, I became a journalist in spite of myself.

As drama critic for the *Morning Post,* a respectable daily, I worked with Bernard Colliers, head of the cultural pages, under the orders of Paul Adler, the all-powerful, respected editor in chief, my bearded professor's former student. When I went to see him in his office, cluttered with newspapers, books, magazines, and other papers, Paul went on correcting a story without giving me so much as a glance. I couldn't help being wary of the man: he had a piercing look and his face was thin and bony; the first impression he gave was of great severity. Later I learned to deal with his mood swings, his impatience, and his tantrums.

"So, young man, it seems you're dying to become a journalist?"

"No. Not a journalist. I wanted to be an actor."

"And like so many others, since you can't do anything else, you're falling back on the glorious profession of journalist."

"No again. It was my professor's idea, not mine."

"I know. He told me."

I kept silent, thinking: nothing is going to come of this. It's a waste of time. A failure from the very start. Why should I have any illusions? This man doesn't like me; it's as clear as daylight. He'll never like me. He's not going to hire me just to please a professor, even if he's the best, most prominent professor around. He's going to dismiss me, promising to get back to me in a few days or a few years.

However, he continued our conversation. "What play have you seen recently, and where? I don't mean a show put on by your friends. I mean real theater, with professionals. On Broadway or Off Broadway."

In a faint voice I replied, "Eugene O'Neill's *The Iceman Cometh.*"

"Did you like it?"

"Yes. A lot."

"Why?"

How could I avoid banalities? I told him that I had

admired the dramatic intensity of the play, the actors' sober performance, the austere direction . . .

"Fine," he said. "Go into the next office. Tell me all this in writing."

How can you write something intelligent and worthwhile under such pressure, when words are buzzing around in your head and your heart is pounding wildly?

I tried, God is my witness, I tried. But I knew it would serve no purpose. It was a losing battle.

Bah, I said to myself, never mind. It's bound to be a slapdash job. What does it matter what I say and how I say it? Let's be quick and move on. A poor student, I stuffed into my "assignment" everything I knew about the author, including the writers he was influenced by: Chekhov, Gogol, Joyce, Kafka—and why not?—the Midrash, and so on. I never wrote anything as mediocre.

A good hour later, I knocked on the boss's door and handed him three typewritten pages, which I hadn't bothered to reread.

He glanced at them and called out to me, "I'm busy right now. I'll get back to you with my opinion tomorrow or the day after tomorrow. Leave me your phone number."

I shared an anxious twenty-four hours with Alika. She was more nervous than I, and more agitated. I knew the response would be negative. She was more optimistic. She tried to calm me and help me pass the time, by drinking, eating, making love with me—I got that out of it at least. But I expected the worst. I was annoyed at myself for having listened to my professor. I shouldn't have gone and disturbed that editor in chief, who was so full of himself; it had been a mistake to expose myself to the ridiculous humiliation he inflicted on me; I'd never forgive myself for it . . .

There was no word from him all day.

A second sleepless night. Alika was fed up and so was I.

You stupid idiot, I said to myself for the tenth time. You let a stranger make a fool of you. Shame on you.

The following morning, Alika popped out to the corner grocery. She reappeared after a few minutes, out of breath.

"Look, Yedi. I bought the newspaper. Look at the first page."

There they were, the opening lines of my piece. And then: "Continued in the Culture pages." A little paragraph announced that the author of this review was the paper's new drama critic and included a rather flattering biographical notice mentioning my bearded professor.

I was just dying to grab a cab to go share my joy with my parents. Alika stopped me.

"They're still asleep."

"They won't mind being woken up."

"Later. First, make love to me."

I would have liked to call my grandfather. He slept very little and rose early. But Alika's desire had priority.

Then I called Itzhak and Orli, Méir and Drora. I pictured their happiness. It was sincere and warmed my heart. Then I went to see my parents.

My father made the following comment: "Do you know the difference between a writer and a journalist? The journalist defines himself by what he says, and the writer by what he doesn't say." Was he happy about my success? I had no idea.

My mother hugged me.

"I'm proud of you, son," she said. "Of course, I still wish you'd been a lawyer."

"A journalist is also a lawyer," my father cut in. "He'll stand up for the defenseless, the poor, the starving, for abused children and unlucky writers: isn't that the lawyer's finest mission? As well as the journalist's?"

In response, I felt I should set him straight.

"That's not the kind of journalist I'm going to be, Father. I'll be writing about theater."

My mother put coffee and cookies on the table. We had a warm, protracted conversation on the role of the press in contemporary society. My father believed that it is impossible to separate the areas of activity of individual men or communities. From the ethical point of view—the only truly significant one—everything is interrelated. Mom chose to see lawyers everywhere. As for me, I pleaded for the sovereignty of theater, its virtues but also its obligations.

Before I left them, my father gave me some advice that

he attributed to an obscure author dating from the time of the Apocrypha whom the mysterious One-Eyed Paritus often claimed as a source of inspiration.

"The person who wants to serve his fellow men, hence the community, hence the individuals who comprise it, must observe the following rules: never flatter powerful men, and never submit to their whims. In other words, my son, never let anyone buy you or frighten you. And then this: if you wish to criticize, start by criticizing yourself; try not to disparage anyone, ever. When your opinion is negative, choose your words carefully so as not to humiliate the person you're criticizing or put him to shame."

My new boss gave me advice that was more or less the same. For on that very day, Paul Adler personally informed me that I was now a member of his staff, with the rights and duties this implied.

My apprenticeship years were sometimes arduous but always stimulating.

I never could have imagined that I'd be able to write a straightforward sentence in the hellish noise of a newsroom, where every journalist thinks he's the only person the reader is waiting for.

Important columnists, breathless reporters who can't waste a minute before writing up the latest news, editorial writers tirelessly pleading with the boss not to cut sentences out of their articles. Shouts to the proofreaders: Check those names! Check those figures! Such was the tantrum-prone little world open to the universe at large that fascinated and infuriated me as a beginner.

The first year, I trembled before handing in my reviews to Bernard Colliers, an oafish, surly, taciturn man; irascible. Never self-confident, rarely satisfied, I feared authority and disapproval. When there was no urgency—in other words, when my piece was to appear in the Saturday or Sunday edition—I wrote at home. Alika helped me. She was my first reader; her reaction was vital to me. However, my editor—or the tyrant, as we called him—usually demanded that my article come out in the next day's early edition. So I would start writing it inside the theater, during intermission, and complete it back in the office.

With time, I became accustomed to the rhythm of newspaper life, both regular and chaotic. A hastily and sloppily written item of political news, a misquote, a paragraph verging on plagiarism, triggered furors—fortunately, nipped in the bud by Paul. Was this the sign and secret of his power? As for me, though I rarely get angry, my temper tantrums don't die down easily. Is it because I never aspired to the tiniest particle of power, except the power every man should exert over himself?

As a general rule, I kept aloof from the jealousies and internal quarrels that plague any business, and even more so in an editorial office whose end product is both essential and ephemeral: its truth lasts only as long as it takes the ink to dry.

Having become close to the boss, I went to great lengths never to overshadow anyone.

True, occasionally some more influential colleague tried to convince me that a play or production, or, more specifically, a friend or girlfriend's performance, was marvelous and deserved to be warmly recommended. I listened patiently and answered that of course I would take his or her opinion into account, but that professional deontology—the word was fashionable at the time—didn't really give me the right or the power to indulge him. All private matters, I said, were beyond my aegis.

Usually, the colleague didn't resent me all that much. If he insisted, I would turn to Paul and discreetly seek his advice. I could rely on his support.

What was most important to me about my profession? The fact that it made my relatives proud. My uncle Méir, my aunt Drora, my grandfather, my parents. Itzhak, too, I hoped. Did my brother envy me? It would have been understandable to me. We'd always had a complicated relationship. I'm never sure my happiness contributes to his. I think that Orli, my sister-in-law, is partly to blame. She tries to be liked by everyone, but I don't get caught up in her game. Is that what irritates her husband?

As for my father, he remains an enigma to me. Is he thinking about those who are absent? Sometimes I look at him and I feel like crying.

When I was studying theater and contemplating devoting my life to it, like Alika and by her side, my father read me the following text (ancient? By a precursor of the medieval thinker One-Eyed Paritus?). To my ears, even today, it still sounds like a premonitory echo of Paul Valéry's beautiful words engraved on the frontispiece of the Palais de Chaillot: "For God, man is Creation's triumph and challenge; he is both worried about him and proud of him. From the cradle to the tomb, life is a path that man alone can brighten or render arid. Life is a laboratory of ideas, dreams, experiences, and it depends entirely on man himself whether he will draw the lessons that will let him rise to the heavens or those that will hurl him into the throes of hell. Hence, life is everything but a theater where the possibility of choosing remains forever limited."

Was my father seeking to discourage me? Make me aware of the trials awaiting me?

It matters little. I have a boundless love for my father. There is a reason: his own father was what we now call a "survivor." He had been wealthy, and in the last year of the war he still had sufficient means to convince three former clients living in different villages to hide his wife and sons. Grandfather alone, victim of a denunciation, was arrested and deported. Miraculously, he survived and, as soon as he could, he emigrated to New York with his family. My mother, who was in America, had a sunny childhood.

And my own childhood? My earliest memories go back to when I was four years old. Before that, nothing. I'm like so many other Jewish children and adolescents in Brooklyn or Manhattan: Jewish school, high school. Sabbath meals.

Holidays. Hanukkah gifts. Summer sun, winter snow. Childhood friends.

The Tragedy? A taboo, forbidden memories. Directly or indirectly, it had affected all our families. Even on my mother's side: so many uncles, aunts, cousins, other relatives had disappeared. We understood obscurely that they were all part of our collective memory. When a man has an arm or a leg amputated, his "phantom limb" still hurts him. This can be applied to the Jewish people; as the great Yiddish poet Chaim Grade said: each of us feels pain for the limbs that are no longer. But what did I know of the concrete experience of that time? Of the denunciations? Of life in the ghetto? Of hunger and crowding? Of the "actions" prior to the deportations? Of the hunting down of children? Of the constant fear of being suddenly separated from one's loved ones? Of the sealed trains bound for the unknown? Of unspeakable suffering? On those rare occasions when my father alluded to it, you had the impression he was recounting events described in his medieval manuscripts, or even more ancient than those. After all, we still commemorate the destruction of the Temple in Jerusalem and the victims of the Crusades on specific dates in the calendar. But is the Tragedy, which we so inadequately call the Holocaust, similar to these dramatic episodes? Would a single day, just one day of the year, be sufficient to honor its memory?

One Saturday afternoon, my father and I found my grandfather at home, sitting at the table, his head in his hands. It was a short time after my grandmother's death.

He was lonely, in deep mourning, and I used to stop by to see him as often as possible. As soon as he saw me, he raised his head and tried to smile at me.

"The human soul, what a labyrinth. I thought I could find my way in it. No. I've lost my bearings. Listen to this: 'An "entertaining" execution was organized in the old city [of Berdichev in Ukraine]: the Germans ordered the old men [Jews] to put on their tallith [prayer shawl] and their tefillin [phylacteries] and deliver a religious service in the old synagogue, praying God to forgive the errors committed against the Germans. They double-locked the synagogue doors and set the building on fire. Another instance of this kind of German "entertainment" is the story of the death of old Aron Mazor, whose profession was ritual butcher. The German officer who looted Mazor's apartment ordered the soldiers to remove everything he had put aside. The officer stayed behind with two soldiers to "entertain" himself: he had found a big butcher's knife and realized what Mazor's profession was. "I want to watch you work," he said and told the soldiers to go fetch the neighbor's three little children.' "

And my grandfather added, "Poor Vassili Grossman, he is great and moving." His narrative stops at this point. He doesn't tell us what happened. Did Mazor obey the order to kill the children? Did he sacrifice himself rather than hurt them? But I'll tell you: Mazor isn't guilty. The Germans are. And I curse them. I will curse them to my dying day. I'll curse them as I weep and as I hold back my tears. I'll curse them by day and curse them by night. I'll curse them in the name of the dead and in the name of the living. I'll curse them for Mazor and for Vassili Grossman.

He put his fists on his eyelids. So I wouldn't see his tears.

Then, after a long silence, he added, "I hope this kind of narrative breaks the Messiah's heart and makes the heavens weep."

As for my father, I rarely saw him weep. Usually when my brother and I lingered at the table after a meal, or in his study, he liked to listen to us with an impassive air. He's a good listener. He says that's the way he is: he expresses himself by listening. The first thing he always taught his students was the art of keeping their ears open. He would look at me, his head tilted and frowning, and I knew not a single word I said escaped him, even if I was telling him about my day at school or the latest baseball game. Sometimes he took advantage of a pause to ask for an explanation, usually with just one word, such as "Why?" or "When?"

My brother Itzhak loves him, too, of course. But in his own way: he loves him and at the same time he's afraid of him, or afraid because of him. He admitted this to me one day. We were adolescents and on our way home from the hospital where our father had undergone elective surgery. "When I see him, my chest becomes heavy with anxiety. And I don't know why," he said. In my case, it's different: when I think of him, I get a lump in my throat. I'm in pain for him.

Since I started working at the newspaper, he had gotten into the habit of reading it more attentively and with greater curiosity than the other dailies. He shares with me his thoughts on given columns. He doesn't particularly like the articles that proclaim their commitment in the name of truth: "The truth of the journalist," he often says, "is not the same as the philosopher's. The former looks for facts, the latter is interested in what transcends facts." When he talks to me about my articles, there's a faint smile in the corner of his mouth. "You don't have this problem. You're concerned with artistic truth. That's *one* truth but not *the* truth."

One day I devoted an article to a play set in an Eastern European ghetto. I was harsh on its author, who had included too many erotic elements in the play for my taste. When I walked into my father's study, he was reading my review. I wondered, Should I ask him what he thinks? The sad look on his face was enough for me. But I still don't know if it was the play or my article that had made him unhappy. Retired, he spent all his time looking for ancient documents related to the Apocrypha, the book of Jubilees, so dear to his father. Nothing gave him greater childlike joy than others showing an interest in it. He was convinced that countless parchments of this kind, perhaps even the "Maccabees," lay buried somewhere in the mountain caves near Jerusalem. Who would be so fortunate as to find them? One day I saw him in seventh heaven: he had just read a book annotated by One-Eyed Paritus. The latter referred to a manuscript titled "The End of Time" dating from the age of the Prophets in Judea. "Look," my father said, jubilantly. "Look at what he says about anger burning the heart whose ashes wait for hatred before being wiped out: 'God alone has the right to feel it; not his creatures.' Or envy, look at what the same Paritus has to say about it: 'Be wary of those who seek to arouse envy: you, reader and student, envy another person's virtues, but not the power or gold he might possess; what shines today will be dust or ashes tomorrow.' "

IT IS BECAUSE OF Werner Sonderberg that, one fine spring day, I found myself in court, in the bosom of the justice system. Not as a lawyer, as my mother had wished, but as an interested observer. And above all as a drama critic.

This was the boss's idea. Rather original, not to say harebrained. To tell the truth, I had tried to dissuade him.

"I haven't studied law, Paul, as you know. I've never attended a trial, and never set foot in a courtroom. Do you want me to make a fool of myself? My area of expertise is theater!"

"That's just it. Trials are *like* theater. All those who participate in them are playing a part. In England, the judges wear wigs. In France it's robes. When the lawyer says, in his client's name, 'we plead guilty or not guilty,' it's as if he himself were guilty or not guilty, too. It's theater, I tell you. In a criminal trial, especially with a jury, there's always suspense and drama. That's why the readers are interested in it."

"And the defendant, Paul?" I replied. "Is it a game, for him, too?"

"It's up to you to tell us."

That's how, from one day to the next, the aforementioned Werner Sonderberg, nephew of Hans Dunkelman, burst into my life.

I remember: a Sunday, late afternoon. I return from the theater and find a meeting of the editors. They're preparing the layout. The Middle East is on the front page as usual, as well as a speech by the president at a midwestern university. Then the secretary of state's televised statement on the subject of bilateral negotiations with Moscow on nuclear disarmament. I listen with only half an ear. My thoughts remain focused on the hapless actors who had to perform in an avant-garde comedy that never took off. Thank God, it won't have a long run. But how can I express this without being nasty? I'm lost in these considerations when I hear voices getting louder. It's Paul losing his temper.

"The trial of the year, as they say, starts next week and we are unprepared?"

"Our two legal reporters are away," says Charles Stone, the old-timer in charge of the metropolitan desk. "James is on vacation and Frederic is getting married."

"Couldn't he pick a better time?"

"Maybe he could have," Charles says, "but not his fiancée. As she sees it, happiness is much more urgent. She's not a journalist."

Contrary to what everyone feared, Paul did not explode. Head bent down, hiding his anger, he started to search in his mind for someone who might fit the bill, and I had no trouble figuring out why he was hesitating. No one appealed to him. So-and-so wrote too slowly; another lacked precision and sparkle; another really had to be kept in his assigned job. And suddenly his eyes met mine.

And that's how I found myself spending hours delving into the archives of our newspaper, looking for material I could use in my first legal column. And after that? Tomorrow is another day. God is great.

Werner Sonderberg is a young German of twenty-four. Born in a town near Frankfurt, he moved with his mother to France, where he attended secondary school. After his mother's death, he came to the United States to get a master's degree in comparative literature and philosophy at New York University. Intelligent, hungry for knowledge, as an uprooted person he made a lot of friends at the university; he was even known to have had a few passing affairs. His teachers treated him kindly and predicted an outstanding career for him in his adopted country. Until then, nothing to report. No police record. No alcohol, no drugs.

One fine morning, a wealthy compatriot, Hans Dunkelman, came to visit him, claiming to be his relative; at the time, Werner didn't understand: Was he an uncle, a distant cousin? His name didn't ring a bell. Strongly built, dressed with meticulous elegance, he must be a wealthy industrialist, an investor or stockbroker, thought the young man.

They were often seen together. So much so that Werner's girlfriend, Anna, a young brunette with cheerful eyes, complained about it to their mutual friends.

"When I want to spend an evening with him," she said, pouting, "I have to make an appointment. I know, he told me, the man is his uncle, the only living member of his family. But still there's a limit, don't you think?"

One day, she couldn't control her anger. "Werner just told me he was going to take time off in the mountains with that Dunkelman. Without me. Take time off from what, from whom? From me maybe? I can't get over it!"

Indeed, Werner and his uncle went to the Adirondacks, not far from the Canadian border, but the nephew returned alone. Taciturn, he refused to answer when Anna quizzed him about his uncle's absence.

"We separated," he finally said by way of explanation, looking annoyed. "That's all. And I hope I never see him again."

"But why? What happened?" asked the young student. "Did you quarrel?"

Werner shrugged his shoulders as if to say, don't harp on it.

Obviously preoccupied, he preferred to remain alone, as

though he felt estranged from love and happiness. Anna tried in vain to make him relax. This was the first time such a thing was happening to them. He seemed cut off from the outside world, impervious to his girlfriend's attentions.

Several days later, alerted by a passing tourist, the local police discovered Hans Dunkelman's corpse at the foot of a cliff. Accident, suicide, or murder? Did he throw himself into the void? Did he succumb to malaise? Did someone push him? The autopsy revealed a high alcohol content in his bloodstream. At the hotel where Werner and he had rented two rooms for a week, they found the name of his nephew, who had returned to New York precipitately.

Two days later, Werner Sonderberg was arrested and charged with murder.

After rereading and correcting my introductory article on the trial, I leave the newspaper office and go home. It is night. Alika welcomes me, looking surprised.

"It's late. What happened?"

I tell her about the turbulent meeting of the editorial staff, but the solution Paul found doesn't please my wife.

"Don't tell me you're giving up the theater."

"Don't be afraid. We'll still be going to all the good plays . . . if and when there are any."

"How are you going to be able to juggle the two issues, writing reviews and summarizing the trial proceedings?"

"No problem: the trial takes place during the day. And it

won't last long. A few days. Maybe a week. That's what everyone says."

"But are you sure you can handle this sort of assignment?"

"No, I'm not. But Paul is sure. You know him; he's stubborn. Once he gets an idea into his head, he won't budge an inch. And he's a friend. I've got to trust him."

Alika is just as obstinate as Paul, and she isn't convinced. But she becomes resigned.

"Let's hope these few days go by quickly . . . and pleasantly."

But the trial would have many surprises in store for us.

Very early the next morning, I'm barely awake when I get a phone call from Paul.

"I read your piece. It's going on the front page. But let me be frank: it's not what I expected of you. You just made a compilation of what others have written. Too many facts, too many details. In a word, too dry. You're not a machine. Think of your passion for the stage. The courses you took. These are the tools you should use. Each person has to come alive, every sentence has to be effulgent, and everything has to revolve around the main character."

"I see. You shouldn't have . . ."

"Don't take it badly. But on reading you, one has the impression that you've never heard of this crime, am I mistaken?"

"No, you're right," I say in a weak voice. "You're always right. But I warned you that . . ."

"That you're not the right man for the job. Yes, I know. You're wrong. Trust me: you can do better and you will."

"I'll try, Professor."

We both hang up at the same time.

"I should have listened to you," I say to Alika, who is still half asleep. "I shouldn't have agreed to it."

"Agreed to what?"

I let her sleep.

First session.

Room number 12 in the New York County Criminal Court is packed. Photographers, reporters, lawyers, legal correspondents, the German consul. They all seem to know one another. Habitués, apparently. They all speak at the same time: the weather, the baseball and football games. The stock market. The latest gossip. I can't make sense of it. I don't know anyone. I don't belong to their world. Estranged from myself, I sit quietly in my corner, pen and pad in hand, my eyes wandering around the setting where a man's future will be hanging in the balance. Will he find freedom again? Will he lose it forever? Will he win back the right to happiness? Will he become a respectable member of the human family again, or remain one of humanity's black sheep? And what about me, what am I doing here? Where do I fit in?

A murmur sweeps through the room. The defendant is brought in; he has been cast in the part of showing how man and act can coincide, and how society judges one of its own.

Flanked by two policemen and wearing a gray suit, a white shirt, and a blue tie, Werner projects the image of an elegant man whom fate has turned into a culprit. His features are drawn, his gestures slow, he has a fixed, lackluster gaze; he doesn't acknowledge a single familiar face—his mind is elsewhere. He walks toward his seat accompanied by his two attorneys, Michael Redford, his court-appointed lawyer, and Peter Coles, a lawyer hired by the German consulate. As the leading man in a scene whose lines he doesn't know, he makes a successful entrance: he is the focus of attention. It is from him that we expect the truth: the explanation for an irreversible act. Is he deliberately adopting an indifferent attitude to his surroundings, to what awaits him? Where do his thoughts lead him? To the scene of the crime, up there in the mountains? Or to his victim, to whom he will be bound to his dying day, no matter what happens? Was it precisely that bond he sought to establish by committing his crime?

"He's so young," someone whispers. "He doesn't look like a murderer," says another. A third person remembers that, after all, he's German. Therefore? You can expect anything.

What is my first impression? Guilty or not guilty? How is one to know? How can one be positive? Yet it is possible he is guilty. Why not? There had been a quarrel, that's certain.

A brusque movement, entirely unpremeditated, and the young man could easily have pushed the old man, even if he later regretted it.

Suddenly my imagination becomes fired up. I see myself with him in another setting. In a train or a café. Two strangers. In the theater? I address him with one word: Why? And he replies: Who appointed you judge?

"Ladies and gentlemen, the court is in session!"

In unison, everyone in the room stands up. Tradition first: the law demands respect. As a result, the defendant is no longer the focus of attention. The presiding judge, Robert Gardner, in his black robe, vested with specific powers whose reach only the habitués understand, is now the focal point. Everyone stares at him with curiosity, as if they were trying to guess the future: Will he be strict or understanding, inflexible or easily swayed?

"Be seated," he says, greeting the court with a nod.

A dry, dispassionate, impersonal voice that speaks not so much for an individual as for a system. This man has only one concern: to forge ahead, rejecting any compromise, or any deviation from the law, which is immutable and incorruptible. The clerk announces that the court is convened in order to examine case number 613-D: *New York State v. Werner Sonderberg.* The judge wants to know if all the participants are present. The answer is yes. The prosecutor, the defendant, the defense lawyers—all are present. Are they all ready? the judge asks. Yes.

The first session is now open. The trial can begin. Suddenly it occurs to me: if you think about it, I've got a part to play here. Much will depend on my articles. The judge may read them. Will he be influenced by my comments?

"Will the defendant please stand up? Kindly state your name, age, place of birth, profession, and place of residence."

"Werner Sonderberg. Twenty-four years old. Born in West Germany. A student at New York University. I've been in America for a year. I live in downtown Manhattan. Thirty-three West Fourth Street."

A slow, calm, precise voice: someone who controls his feelings. He'll know how to defend himself. My thoughts wander and take me to the distant past: if he had lived in the dark times, he would have worn a uniform—but which one? I immediately stop myself: I have no right to imagine him in any uniform. Who appointed me judge?

"Enter your plea: guilty or not guilty?"

A required question in the United States. Usually it produces no emotion in the courtroom. The defendant hesitates a second before raising his voice as if he wished to convey a tone of gravitas and replies, "Guilty."

He stops to catch his breath. Stifled murmurs on the benches. Some members of the audience are clearly disappointed. After this admission, no dramatic developments can be expected. Or eloquent attacks.

" . . . and not guilty," the defendant hastens to add.

Surprised, not to say shocked, some observers lean forward to scrutinize the young German's face: in this courtroom, no such statement has ever been heard before. Judge Gardner raises his hand to call the court to order.

"This is not an acceptable answer. It is my duty to inform the defendant that the law requires him to answer guilty or not guilty."

The attorney stands up and takes the floor in order to speak for his client.

"Your Honor, will the court allow me to provide an item of information in order to clarify?"

"Mr. Redford, you're a member of the bar and the procedure holds no secrets for you. Might you have forgotten, for some extraordinary reason, to tell your client that the court allows a plea of guilty or not guilty, but not the two simultaneously?"

"I did make that clear to my client, Your Honor. But he persists in . . ."

"Mr. Redford, let's leave the explanations for later. At present, let's have the defendant tell us in an audible, intelligible voice whether he pleads guilty or not guilty."

Werner shakes his head.

"So it's no?" asks Judge Gardner. "Not guilty?"

The attorney whispers a few words into his client's ear. Then: "Please forgive us, Your Honor, but my client only wished to tell the court that no, he can't accept the choice, because . . ."

"In that case," the judge rules, showing his irritation, "the court will decide for him. Clerk, enter a not guilty plea for the defendant."

After that, he motions to the defense attorneys and the prosecutor to come closer.

"I expect to see you in my chambers without delay," he says to them with an intimidating look and in a muffled voice. The hearing is suspended. The court was to reconvene at two p.m.

I run to the newsroom and walk into Paul's office without knocking: as luck would have it, he's with Charles Stone.

"So, how's our legal reporter's baptism going?" Paul asks.

"Talk about experiences, this sure is one," I say. "You're right, it's theater, but in a category of its own. Everyone is improvising, more or less, including the judge. Every kind of surprise is allowed. And I feel like an intruder."

I tell them about my first court hearing. Paul smiles.

"You don't hold it against me that I forced you into volunteering?"

"It's too early to answer yes or no."

"Beware, you sound like your young defendant."

"Except I haven't killed anyone. Not even in my theater reviews."

"I'm waiting for your piece," Charles interjects. "I need it by eight p.m."

"I'll tell Judge Gardner to hurry up."

I go home to have lunch with Alika. She seems displeased with my excitement.

"Don't forget, your first love is theater, after all, not law."

"My first love is you."

"Come and eat."

The afternoon session is devoted to the selection of the twelve-person jury, men and women.

They begin by drawing lots: a peculiar lottery. Each potential juror is presented for approval to the prosecution and the defense. All members of the jury are required to be objective, neutral, devoid of prejudices, and incapable of being moved by anything but reason, a sense of equity and truth. A saint would fit the description.

One of the first potential jurors is an elderly Jewish tailor who is probably religious as he is wearing a yarmulke. In order to get rid of him, the prosecutor questions him on his attitude toward Germany and the Germans.

"Do you think you can be completely objective with respect to the defendant?"

"Why wouldn't I be?"

"Because you're probably attached to the past of your people."

"So? Why would my loyalty to the past cloud my judgment in this particular case?"

"Because you're you and the defendant is who he is."

"You mean I'm Jewish and he's German, which should predispose me to hate him, is that it?"

"No, no, that's not what I meant."

"Fortunately, sir. Because I happen to be against the

principle of collective guilt. Whether German or Muslim, only criminals are guilty; the children of murderers are children, not murderers."

Dismissed.

As for the attorney Michael Redford, he makes use of his right to dismiss two prospective jurors peremptorily.

The next person to be considered is an elegantly dressed woman, in her early forties, intelligent, and wearing light makeup. For some reason, I see her as the wife of a banker, as a lover of Greek and Roman art and of contemporary music. The prosecutor objects to her and dismisses her.

Three sessions will be required for the judge to finalize the jury selection. For the other reporters these sessions are uninteresting, rather repetitive, and devoid of surprises. Not for me. Each one is a discovery leading to a confrontation between the defendant and the eight men and four women sitting in the jury box, to the left of the judge's platform. I have trouble taking my eyes off Werner Sonderberg as I try to guess what he is feeling. After all, his life is in the hands of these individuals more than in those of the judge. He knows—his lawyers have told him—that the vote of the jury has to be unanimous for him to be convicted. All that's needed is one dissenting voice and he can walk away free. I wonder who among the jurors might save him. Astonishingly, he seems preoccupied by something else entirely. He seems indifferent to the jury.

But then what is he thinking of with a look of such concentration?

My first articles seem to be well received.

"You see? I was right," Paul remarks. "It's because you have no understanding of legal issues that you succeed in making the reader interested. You connect on a dramatic, personal level."

Charles agrees. "There's a freshness in your writing that you don't find in the articles of veteran court reporters."

"Let's talk shop," I say. "Every hearing reminds me of a theatrical performance. I try to bring to light the dramatic tension that will make the performance progress but at an unhurried pace. As in theater, I feel the tension must come from within and be devoid of obvious artifice."

"Except that in the theater," Paul says in his low voice, "the actors and the audience go home, safe and sound, after the curtain comes down each day. In any case, I notice you're interested in your new field of activity. Maybe even more than in the theater?"

That evening I recount the conversation to Alika as we walk to a nearby restaurant for dinner.

"Paul's wrong," I say to her.

She doesn't respond.

"You don't believe me? You have doubts about my loyalty?"

"As I always do. You know me."

"Even in this instance?"

"Even in this instance."

"And why?"

"Because I've read your articles."

"And? What do they prove?"

"They're good. Better than your theater reviews."

"Thanks for the compliment. But let's say that I work differently. I didn't know anything about the judiciary world. I never thought about it. But, you know, you can feel attracted to something that's foreign to you."

"That's possible."

I don't understand. Why is she so irritated?

"Do you actually think that because I'm suddenly interested in the law I'm going to forsake the theater?"

"I don't know what to think anymore."

"Do you want me to give it up?"

"It's what you want that counts."

"Me, I want to understand why you're annoyed at me. Am I a journalist or not? I have to go where my editors send me. Let's say tomorrow I'm assigned to a local police station. I can't just say no. The same goes for this trial."

Alika knits her brows, furious and seemingly hurt.

"That's completely different. In a police station, you'd do your work and you might even do it well, but you wouldn't love it. Whereas as far as this trial goes, you enjoy attending it. Enjoy talking about it. Enjoy showing off your talent. And your new passion. That's the point: we no longer share the same passion."

"You're mistaken."

"Well, then, prove it to me: return to theater."

"How many times do I have to keep saying it? When I'm in the courtroom, that's exactly where I am—at the theater!"

"Really? Who's the author of the play? The judge? The defendant? The public? Don't tell me they're improvising, all of them as long as they're . . ."

"Yes, they are, in a way."

"You're out of your mind!"

This is our first real quarrel. There will be others—more or less futile, more or less serious. In her opinion, I'm spending too much time away from home. My explanations—the fact that I'm no longer in control of my schedule because of the trial, the interviews with lawyers and spectators, my library research and editorial meetings—are useless. She criticizes anything I say. "Even when you're here, which is increasingly rare, you're miles away."

I don't understand what's happening to us. For the first time in ages, we're getting on each other's nerves. There are a lot of silences. Misunderstandings. Some discoveries: the little gestures that used to awaken or strengthen our love now dampen it. My way of buttoning my shirt. Her way of wiping her lips when she drinks her coffee. The magic is gone.

Actually, Alika is not entirely wrong to be annoyed with me. I've undergone a change. Just a week ago, she occupied all my thoughts and filled my life, whereas, for the last few days, the trial has suddenly become the focus of all my attention. But she's also mistaken: I haven't forgotten my passion for the stage.

In fact, after our quarrels, I set a rule for myself: to go to the theater at least once a week, though Alika goes almost every evening. And this while continuing her studies. According to her, our professor and protector shares her apprehensions about me.

"He wonders," she says one day, returning from a performance, "if you would still be able to write an objective review of a play in which I would be playing one of the leads."

"I have no idea."

"But do you think that could happen?"

A shudder goes down my spine: I remember *The Three Sisters.* Alika with a group of students, in a small amateur theater. Does she know? I don't let myself get flustered.

"No doubt it could."

"And so? What would you do?"

"You're right, and so is the professor: it would be a problem for me. But maybe not for the reason you think. I would say to myself: if I like it, people will say it's because of you. And if my review is critical, the people who don't like me will snigger: look at that bastard, he's humiliating his own wife."

"So? How would you get out of this dilemma?"

"This is not about to happen tomorrow, as far as I know. We have time to think about it."

But, to tell the truth, I'd rather not think about it.

When my grandfather read my articles, he said: "Long ago, in Judea, in the days when the Temple still stood in Jerusalem, a twenty-three-member court would sit and deliberate in cases requiring capital punishment. If the sentence was unanimous, it was immediately thrown out of court: it was inconceivable that, among the twenty-three judges, not one would side with the poor defendant, who was alone and helpless in facing them."

I told him that I wished I could have attended those trial deliberations and covered them for the newspaper at the time.

"Remember the lesson, my son: when a man's life is at stake, it is not theater."

It is day three of the proceedings. The experts at the courthouse are predicting the trial will be relatively short. Not many witnesses will be called to the stand. According to the prosecution, at the fateful moment, the defendant and his uncle were alone. No one saw Hans Dunkelman die. Going by what they call "circumstantial evidence," provided by the local police, he fell from the heights of a plateau. But the question is, as we know: Was it an accident or a murder? The nephew's ambiguous statement is disturbing and preys on everyone's mind. How can someone be both guilty *and* not guilty? The young German remains silent while the other protagonists reveal themselves to be nonstop talkers. In a tribunal everyone wants to be heard. The only one who doesn't seem to care is the main character, about whom there is so much curiosity that men and women have jammed the courtroom. From the very first hearings, I wondered: Will he even take the trouble to listen? He seems absent to the public and to himself.

On the fourth day, I describe my impressions of Sonderberg to Paul.

"He's someone who is engaged in a struggle, and I don't know against whom or what."

"Against fear?"

"Perhaps."

"If he's guilty, he could get the death penalty or, at minimum, life imprisonment. That's a good enough reason to be afraid, isn't it?"

"Yes. But there's something else; I sense it. Put it down to the kind of intuition that theater teaches you to cultivate. At a certain point, he looked at a woman in the jury. I caught his gaze. And his fleeting smile. As though he thought that if the twelve members of the jury had been women, his sentence would have been to make love to each of them."

"A swaggering smile?"

"I don't know. I think he was trying to destabilize her. But, for a second, he succeeded in destabilizing me."

Paul, lost in his thoughts, says nothing.

To my amazement, the readers seem to like what I write. I see the hearings as a series of acts in the course of which the characters come onstage one after the other. Each session begins with the curtain going up; each adjournment is like an intermission. When the clerk tells the public to rise, it is like stage business; all the participants play their part and I play mine.

In this kind of production, any plot development is theoretically possible—and for journalists, desirable—up until the final scene. Let me remind you of the law: if just one jury member has doubts about the defendant's absolute guilt, the defendant is immediately acquitted.

Here again, my grandfather is right: in ancient Judea, it was more practical, though no less complicated. In the Sanhedrin, as I said earlier, if just one jury member ruled in favor of the defendant's innocence, the guilty verdict of the majority prevailed. The defendant no doubt prayed that if one sage out of the twenty-three judges believed in his innocence, he would join the others and support a unanimous guilty verdict, so that his innocence could triumph.

I look around the courtroom. As earlier, I continue to familiarize myself with the surroundings and the ambience. The judge, the prosecutor, the attorneys, the defendant, the clerk: each makes his presence known in his own way, depending on his personality. As for the jury members, their part seems to be that of a mute choir: ill at ease, as if wondering why they're here instead of at work in their offices or spending the day with their family. What would my uncle Méir say if he were on the jury? Or my grandfather?

True, the judge explained to the winners of this lottery that they were performing their duty as citizens, for every individual has the right to be judged by his peers; however, the judge can't stop their minds from wandering.

His peers? Does Werner see them as such? I remind myself that they include a distinguished-looking black woman who is a university professor; a Puerto Rican taxi driver; a woman who is a department store employee; a grandmother of Irish descent; a black man who works on Wall Street (banker, stockbroker, consultant?). They have no names, just numbers. They will sit in the same seats every day, in an order established by the court clerk. With time, they will each adopt a distinctive behavior and body language, and display individual character traits. But initially they form a tight-knit group. They move in unison, turning their heads to the right or to the left, to follow what is going on before the judge, or to scrutinize the defendant's impassive face.

The prosecutor, Sam Frank, is a former marine officer. Tall, slender, a steely look in his eyes, jerky in his gestures, he approaches the trial as if it were a military operation. Werner is the enemy. He is to be unmasked, crushed, and rendered harmless forever in a dark, stifling cell.

Nothing remains here of the old British traditions whereby the different sides wear wigs and caps and question one another with feigned, excessive courtesy, exchanging titles and compliments as they aim their poisoned arrows all the more skillfully. In our courtrooms, no one feels intimidated in expressing himself.

Alternately addressing the judge and the jury, Frank presents the prosecution's case forcefully and with conviction. For him, there are no possible grounds for doubt: Werner Sonderberg is guilty of the murder of his uncle Hans Dunkelman.

"This will be demonstrated to you in the course of this trial, which, we hope, will not be too drawn out. To me, it seems the situation could not be clearer. The young Werner Sonderberg and his elderly uncle Hans Dunkelman leave Manhattan and check into a quiet hotel in the Adirondacks. For one week. Presumably to talk to each other and rest. Did they quarrel? Yes. A chambermaid will confirm the fact. She heard their shouts. The night porter as well. The following day they were seen leaving the hotel together. For a walk. To breathe the cool mountain air. What happened up there in the mountains? What did they say to each other? At which point did their words become unduly violent? Which one struck the other first? Who pushed whom? There's only one possible answer to that last question, since it was the uncle's body that was found by the police. What more do you need? Isn't that enough for you? Very well. His nephew, the defendant, went back to the hotel. Alone. And a short time later, he was alone, at home, in his Manhattan apartment."

He breaks off. A dramatic pause. Turning to the jury, he

gives them a meaningful look. "The prosecution feels there is nothing to add. Besides, you heard him: he admitted he was guilty. So you know who Hans Dunkelman's murderer is. He is here before you. He should be judged in your soul and conscience. Give him the punishment he deserves."

As though obeying him, the jury members look at Werner. So do I. He is sitting upright, head held high; he doesn't react. What are his feelings? What does he see right now? His uncle? He wears a mask of indifference on his face, as though he didn't care about anything. As though his future had fallen apart, his hope had vanished in a final act of violence, along with the life of an old man who had been part of his family.

For a second, I think I see a flutter in Werner's eyes; he seems to be looking for someone in the public. It lasted only a second, and I really have no way of knowing if it was an involuntary movement or a signal directed at a specific person. But thanks to that twinkling of the eye, I located one young woman who is intently watching him with an expression that is hard to define. Later on, I will find out that her name is Anna. I don't know why, but I'm immediately interested in her. So different from Alika. She is attractive, but not in the same way; you look at Alika and you feel like hearing her talk. Not this woman; you gaze at her as if she were a work of art, and it's sufficient. Elegant, haughty in spite of her youth. A sober charcoal gray suit. A blue scarf. A beautiful oval face, tinted glasses, long dark hair that cascades down her back.

"The counsel for the defense may now speak," says the judge.

Michael Redford stands up. Everything about him seems exaggerated. A heavy head on sturdy shoulders. Long arms, large hands. Puffy lips, bushy eyebrows. After greeting the court, he turns to the jury and scrutinizes them silently for a moment, as if to warm them up or prepare them for what they are about to hear.

"Ladies and gentlemen of the jury, at the start of this trial I have very little to say to you, except this: Werner Sonderberg has pleaded not guilty for the simple reason that he's innocent. He didn't kill his uncle; he didn't kill anyone. He is incapable of killing. We intend to prove this to you. To begin with, our purpose is to demonstrate to you that the prosecution has no tangible proof on which to base their case. Its argument is built on hazy assumptions. Now let me ask you to stop looking at me. Instead, look at my client, Werner, who came to America to build a future for himself. He is not known to have enemies, whether at the university or elsewhere. A superior student, absorbed in his work, his life plan did not include murder, no matter what the prosecution says: it sees him as guilty and would like to make him pay the price. He went to the mountains to spend a few days with a man who introduced himself to him as his uncle. One morning, they went for a walk. Werner Sonderberg came back to the hotel alone. That very night he returned to his studio apartment. Did his uncle, who stayed behind, fall to his death? Did he commit suicide? We have no idea, nor do the police. In fact, they should have conducted more of an in-depth inquiry before making an arrest. In a democracy like ours, we don't arrest an innocent man just because we have no other suspects. Werner Sonderberg has no business being here. That's our deep conviction."

Slowly, imperceptibly, he moves closer to the young defendant, no doubt in order to establish a kind of complicity between them, as though they were one. Bravo, maestro. He knows his job and, as far as I can tell, is performing it to perfection. The twelve members of the jury keep their eyes riveted on him as he returns to his seat. Some of them seem intrigued, others interested. Two among them, however, have to struggle not to show their boredom.

What if I were one of them? What if the fate and honor of this young German were in my hands? A dangerous, dishonest thought: it would lead me where I won't allow myself to tread. Like that other bizarre thought that crosses my mind: could I possibly be the one in the dock? Could I be, as he is, the murderer of an old German, a witness to those horrible times? A participant even? I quickly dismiss the thought. I'm not Werner Sonderberg. Or his double.

I'm me.

I keep thinking about my grandfather and his memories: What would he have advised me? What opinion would he have had of that young German? He's far away but I wish he were present. I learned so much from him. I didn't realize it at the time, but now I do, so much so that it makes me suffer.

I think of my father, too. I'd like to know what he thinks of Werner Sonderberg.

One day, when I was still very young, I was feeling a sadness verging on depression, and talking to no one because a friend had betrayed my trust. My father invited me into his study. As usual, he was bent over a dusty book. I stood behind him so I could read what he was pointing to.

"It's a text by the great Rabbi Kalonymus ben Aderet. He lived in Barcelona and later in Fez. He was the contemporary and friend of One-Eyed Paritus and translated some of his poems into Sanskrit. Here he makes us reflect on man's secret powers: man did not light the sun, but it is he who measures everything by its light; he did not invent the darkness of night, but it is he who fills it with his nostalgic songs; he did not vanquish death, but it is he who stands up to it with each breath and each prayer. A speck of dust, he knows how to rise above the stars in order to get near to his Creator's creation."

My father went on, without changing his tone of voice. "Remember, my son. It's not me talking to you right now; it's this great poet and visionary, close to Don Itzhak Abrabanel, who had to leave Catholic Spain in 1492 because he wanted to remain true to our alliance with God. It is he who is telling you not to despair."

My father read a few passages in silence before speaking

again with the same gentle and solemn tone, and the same slow and melancholic rhythm.

"And Rabbi Kalonymus ben Aderet also has this to say to you: 'Today, on the eve of the Sabbath, I am strolling under the blue and tender sky of Italy. We have found a land of welcome here. We live among ourselves in the ghetto and study the Law of Moses so that it will guide us to Jerusalem step-by-step. True, we are not free, but we dream of true freedom; we are not happy, but our souls sing of the joy of being able to remember the sunlit times of David and Solomon, and Isaiah's and Jeremiah's heartrending appeals to justice and generosity. In spite of everything we have been through, we are still capable of gratitude here; our most beautiful texts are those expressing our gratitude.' Follow me on my path: look at that Jewish man and that boy; it is a father taking his son to school; look at that woman and her smile; her mind is on all those of whom she is the descendant; look at that old man: he is smiling, in the distance, at the adolescent he used to be, the adolescent who accompanies him to a future whose promise is a ray of sunshine. How can we see all this and not cry out: Thank you, Lord, for having created a world where human happiness is close to divine grace."

I love my father. I want him to know that. For all time.

Alika and I went to Long Island for a few days, to the home of her friends Alex and Emilie Bernstein, who are both movie actors. We needed it. Our relationship has become increasingly tense and strained. If it seems like we still understand each other, it's because we hardly speak to each other. As soon as I utter a sentence I know it will be misunderstood. I need only give an opinion for it to trigger in my wife a reaction that's not only offended but offensive. This isn't her fault or mine. It's life. Passionate love is for adolescents. We've outgrown that phase.

The first day begins without incident: the gods are protecting us. We take our meals together, and Emilie, curious by nature, asks what we have on our minds these days.

"The politics of the American administration," Alex proclaims. "It's appalling. The whole world is against us. You need only go to Europe to become aware of it."

"Whereas for me, it's the theater, of course," Emilie says.

"Whereas I'm troubled by both these things," Alika replies.

"Whereas for me," I say, "I deplore the fact that the two are linked. The politics of theater is as sickening as the theater of politics."

"There, that's who I have to live with," Alika replies, "a punster."

They all laugh. And we change the subject. I withdraw into my shell.

At dinner, we are joined by an Anglo-French couple. We talk about journalism. Is it useful to a democratic society? Honest or corrupt like everything else? A reliable source of information, a necessary tool for forming an opinion? Emilie and I stand up for the media, primarily because they represent an indispensable element in protecting individual and collective liberties. Alika is our most violent opponent. I've rarely seen her as fierce in her opinions. For her, even the best daily papers disgrace their readers. And she goes on to quote and appropriate the remark of a big British press baron concerning a well-known magazine: "It isn't what it used to be . . . and actually it never was." And this applies to all publications, she tries to convince us, with no exceptions. Alex agrees with her. So do their guests. Emilie and I valiantly stand up to them. Alika flares up.

"How can the two of you stick up for all those miserable newspapers and weeklies? I'm prepared to think you don't read them! Even the cultural pages are overpoliticized. As for the literary supplements, what do they tell us except 'long live the buddy-buddy network'? What kind of moral rectitude is that? And what about the right to truth?"

I admit I'm surprised. I didn't expect this flow of haughty words from her mouth. Clearly we're not in the same camp anymore.

Calm and resolute, Emilie pursues her counterattack and cites the facts: Can we really suspect such and such a writer, at such and such a newspaper, of dishonesty? And can we honestly question the integrity of such and such a professor, who writes in such and such a journal?

Without the slightest compunction, Alika answers with a shrug of the shoulders. "Yes we can. And we should."

"In other words," Emilie says, "they're all guilty until proven innocent, is that it?"

"No," Alika concedes. "I wouldn't go that far. But I maintain that, as a reader, I have the right to wonder about their conception of ethics."

After the meal, we retire to our bedroom. It is late. I feel like sleeping. But I know I won't get to sleep. Alika is angry. If I understand correctly, she feels I shouldn't have challenged her views.

"You allied yourself with Emilie. You make a lovely couple."

"Don't be silly. Are you jealous?"

"No . . . Yes . . . I resent you for ruining our stay here."

"Because I'm of the same opinion as Emilie about one specific point?"

"No, because you're closer to her than to me."

"To her? Of course not. Only to some of her ideas."

"In the past we used to agree on every subject."

"There were some we had never talked about. Proof is . . ."

"In the past, you loved me."

"And now?"

"Now you love me less. And differently."

"Don't tell me you think I'm in love with Emilie!"

"No. I just think you could be. And that you don't love me the way you used to."

A pregnant silence. A restless night. We each stay on our own side of the bed.

ON THE SUBJECT OF JEALOUSY . . .

Enter the beautiful and fearsome Kathy, one of the secretaries from the cultural pages: a svelte, lithe brunette in her early thirties, with wavy hair and gleeful eyes, she is outspoken and a malicious gossip. She is a workaholic who loves to complain of being treated as a slave (by herself?). According to rumor—a rumor she believes, perhaps rightly—half the men on the editorial staff are madly in love with her. And she loves to joke around about it.

"Oh," she often sighs, "all these broken hearts . . ."

I've been one of her favorite targets for a long time. She never ceases to provoke me, perhaps because I'm not in her circle of suitors. She calls me the "ascetic," and I have neither the courage nor the desire to set her straight.

One evening, I return from the trial and think I'm alone in my office. I set to work on my article when I feel a hand on my shoulder. It's Kathy. She's come from upstairs where the editors are preparing the layout for the literary supplement.

"Tell me you're in love with me."

“I hate lies.”

“Well, then, tell me you love me a little.”

“Why should I?”

“Because I could use it.”

I could reply that I could use someone saying that to me, too, but I prefer to cut the conversation short.

“I have to finish this piece. Afterward I’ll tell you whatever you want to hear.”

“I have time. I’ll wait for you.”

I know that Alika will be coming home late tonight: she’s attending the rehearsal of a play directed by a girlfriend.

“I’m working on my third draft. I’m afraid I’ll still be at it for a good hour.”

“Show it to me.”

Still standing, she grabs my pages, frowns as she reads them, picks up a pen, makes a few corrections, and hands them back.

“Here’s your article. Now it’s good.”

She’s right, of course.

“As a reward, let’s get a cup of coffee.”

“Okay. Where should we go?”

“Well, what about my place?”

I look at her, stunned.

“You know full well that I’m not free, that I’m married.”

“There’s nothing I don’t know about you. But don’t be afraid: I don’t intend to take your virginity.”

“Too bad,” I say.

We burst out laughing. I’m embarrassed; she’s impertinent. Then we leave the editorial offices. Her apartment isn't very far away. We walk there.

It's a spring evening, calm and bright. The sidewalks are congested with students in shirtsleeves. The restaurants and a number of shops are still open. What would Alika say if she suddenly encountered us? It's best not to think about it. Besides, we've arrived.

"I live on the sixth floor. Should we wait for the elevator? It's pretty slow."

"Let's walk up."

Kathy is more energetic than I am. I struggle as I follow her up. Hers is a modest apartment, tastefully furnished. Living room, kitchen, and bedroom. I flop down on the couch, out of breath. I ask her if she knows the story about Sarah Bernhardt; she lived on the ground floor when she was young and on the fifth floor when she was old. "I've always wanted a man's heart to race when he comes to see me," she used to say.

"I'm not old yet," says Kathy. "And if your heart is thumping, let me hear it."

"You're not a physician, as far as I know."

"But I might be a healer."

She brings us coffee and sits down next to me.

"What are you thinking about? Your article?"

"No. I'm thinking about Werner."

"The murderer?"

"The young man accused of murder."

"Why are you thinking about him right now and not about me?"

"I'm wondering whether you would make love to him if you saw him smile."

"A weird question. People often say there's an erotic component in every act of murder. If you want, if I have the opportunity, I'm prepared to experiment, as we used to say in college. And I'll get back to you with the results."

"In this particular instance, theory will do. I'm not interested in the practical applications."

Kathy puts her cup down on the table and, while scrutinizing me at length with an amused look, sharply cross-examines me in a mocking tone.

"We've known each other for quite some time, my friend. You've never courted me; you avoid me. Actually, you're not my type; don't worry: I'm not trying to seduce you, but I find you interesting. I look at you. I observe you. You intrigue me. You live in your own world; strangers are not welcome. Agitated, nervous, tormented: you're never satisfied, never happy. Why do you remain so closed, stubborn, insensitive to warmth and the beauty of the world? Why do you turn down simple pleasures? Why do you reject what is offered to you? Why do you cling to your solitude? It's as if you see danger, or an enemy, in every woman. And betrayal in every moment of joy. Why? I'd like to understand."

What could I answer?

I didn't expect this verbal avalanche with solemn overtones coming from Kathy. Usually she expresses herself more flippantly and insouciantly. Does she ever speak this bluntly with other colleagues on the paper? Is she doing me a favor? To tell the truth, even if I don't want to admit it to myself, I was prepared for something completely different, the beginning of a flirtation perhaps, even if it meant warding her off as far as possible. Yes, I was ready for that. Am I disappointed? By her analysis of my personality, or by her saying that I wasn't her type? After all, Kathy is attractive. And sensual. Should I have made the first move?

"Why do you behave as though you care about me?"

"Because you're remote," she replies, "and remoteness attracts me. Because you're a stranger—at any rate for me. A strange stranger."

Suddenly I think of Alika, who would soon be coming home. I look at Kathy, a gaze fraught with remorse.

"All your questions, I can't answer them. Besides, this isn't a good time."

"You mean you'll answer some other time?"

"Maybe."

"When?"

"I don't know. I have to get home. But before I go, do you know the touching story of the two drops of water . . ."

I cut myself off.

"Two drops of water?" She urges me on.

"That talk to each other. One says: How about going off to seek adventure and discover the immensity of the sea? 'Let's go,' says the other. An eternity later, they meet on my table. You understand? For them, a glass of water is the ocean."

I head toward the door. She walks over and opens it. And there, on the threshold, driven by the desire for forbidden fruit, I kiss her. Will she try to detain me? If she makes the slightest attempt, will I join her? And make Alika wait? And punish her?

Kathy lets me leave. True, I'm not her type. End of episode? Unless fate decides to add another chapter. But is she *my* type? And what about Alika? Let's not think about it anymore. As the proverb my grandfather liked to cite goes: What reason fails to accomplish, time will accomplish.

Actually, when it comes to women, I don't have an easy time. Like children choosing a future profession, for a long time I suffered from chronic indecision. I used to flit from one woman to another, without their realizing it. One day the woman of my dreams was blond; the next, she was dark-haired. Sometimes somber, sometimes sensual. Arrogant in the morning, seductive in the evening.

I have to confess, or at least wonder: if Alika and I have stayed together for so long, perhaps it's because, as she's in theater, she manages to incarnate all women, even women who don't resemble her in the least.

And now, has the time come to change the part, the play, or the tableau? To bring down the curtain? Deep down, I know the answer: we're only at intermission. I'm very attached to Alika. I'd like to get old by her side. She doesn't like my articles on the trial, but she'll come to accept them.

To tell the truth, for the first time in years, I feel good in my new position. Thanks to the trial, for the last few days my name has been on the front page. People talk about me. They're interested in my opinion. Colleagues, both unfamiliar and familiar, acknowledge me as one of them. Suddenly I've become—for how long?—a "member of the brotherhood," a key player. Has the newspaper taken the place of my wife in my life?

Back in the courtroom. Jury and lawyers, prosecutor and witnesses: the entire dramatis personae are present. Elisabeth Whitecomb, the receptionist in the Mountain Hotel, a chubby but pretty woman, clearly glad to be the center of attention for so many onlookers, describes her brief contacts with the defendant in a prudent and solemn tone of voice. He was wearing a dark gray suit. He seemed more like a young teacher than a student. He looked intelligent, calm. Not very talkative, but courteous.

The prosecutor: "He was alone when you saw him?"

Elisabeth Whitecomb bites her lips in order to better concentrate. "Not at the beginning of his stay. He was with an older man. Someone who looked like a senior official or an industrialist. Wealthy, you could see that from his suit. It was Hans Dunkelman. His uncle. Polite, mannered."

"How did you know he was the defendant's uncle?"

"The defendant told me."

"How did it come up?"

"He requested two rooms. One for himself, one for his uncle."

"What did you think of him?"

"He made a good impression on me. Friendly. Cultured. Good manners."

"And the uncle?"

"Impatient. Withdrawn. He let his nephew do the talking. He kept his mouth shut."

"You showed them their rooms?"

"Only the uncle's. The nephew wanted to be sure he liked it. For his own, he just took the keys."

"When did they arrive?"

"I told the inspectors: May twenty-eighth."

"In the morning or in the afternoon?"

"In the early afternoon. They were hungry. I told them to hurry because the restaurant would be closing."

"Did they go there?"

"Not right away. They went to freshen up first."

"Did they come downstairs together?"

"No. The nephew . . . excuse me, the defendant came downstairs in about five minutes, his uncle a bit later."

"Did you chat with the defendant?"

"Yes."

"What about?"

"About the weather, of course. That's the subject that all our guests are interested in. Without exception."

"Did you ask him where he was from?"

"I already knew. From New York. Manhattan."

"How did you know?"

"I read his form, of course!"

"And his uncle's, too?"

"Yes."

"What did it say?"

"That he lived in Germany."

Methodically, the prosecutor guides his witness to the conclusions he wants to reach.

"For how long had they intended to stay at the hotel?"

"The room was booked for a week. That's our rule. You can't book for shorter stays."

"And how long did they stay? The entire week?"

"No. Only three days."

"And then?"

"Then what?"

"When did you see them for the last time?"

"Together? On the thirty-first. In the morning. They went for a walk in the mountains. I told them to be careful. There are dangerous spots. You can slip and fall into the ravine."

"How did they respond?"

"The nephew . . . excuse me, the defendant thanked me."

"And then?"

"They probably didn't take my advice. Next thing you know, the uncle is dead."

"Could you please repeat what you just said?"

"All of it?"

"Just the last sentence, concerning the defendant."

"Well, the uncle is dead."

"Murdered."

"Yes, murdered."

"How do you know?"

"It's what you just said."

"Did you see the defendant again?"

"Yes."

"When?"

"On the same day. A few hours later. He came to get his luggage."

"You must have been surprised."

"At the time I thought his uncle had probably decided to continue his walk on his own. They had taken sleeping bags and food with them. I had a feeling they planned to spend the night in the mountains. Students sometimes do that."

"And the defendant didn't talk to you?"

"He went straight up to his room. He looked calm."

"Though his uncle was already dead."

"I didn't know that yet."

"But he did," the prosecutor shouted. "His behavior didn't surprise you?"

Michael Redford, the lawyer for the defense, stands up and objects. "Your Honor, the prosecutor is out of bounds! He is soliciting the witness and dictating her remarks . . ."

The judge rules in his favor. The prosecutor has to take back his question.

"Very well. So, the defendant came back alone. Did he talk about his walk?"

"No. He just asked me for the bill. He added that he had to shorten his stay and return to Manhattan."

"He didn't explain why?"

"No. He paid with his credit card, got a taxi, and left."

"Did you notice anything strange about his behavior?"

"He seemed in a hurry to leave."

"Was he less courteous? Nervous? Anxious? Troubled?"

"Just as polite as before. But eager to leave."

"That's what you thought at the time. But now, knowing the charges brought against the defendant, does anything come to your mind? A detail? An unusual move on his part? A sign? A comment that could suddenly have another meaning?"

Aware of the importance of the question, the receptionist reflected for a long time before saying, "I thought he looked sad."

"Sad? What do you mean, sad?"

"Sad and disoriented. Like a lost child far away from home."

"It's normal for a man who has just committed a despicable crime to feel sad—is that what you're trying to imply?"

"No. What I mean is when I found out about all this, all the charges against him, I remembered that he looked like a child filled with great sadness. Crushed by an obscure sadness, you could say."

"Well, I maintain that's exactly what a well-educated

young man, from a good family, feels when he's discovered he's a murderer."

Satisfied with his conclusion, the prosecutor turns to the jury and says, "I have no more questions for this witness."

He walks back to his seat and whispers a few words to his assistant, sitting to his left. She nods her head and smiles while the judge turns to the defense.

"And what about you, sir? Do you wish to cross-examine the prosecution's witness?"

"Yes, I would, Your Honor. With the court's permission I'd like to . . ."

"Not now," the judge interrupts him. "After lunch."

During this entire scene, Yedidyah kept watching the defendant, who never betrayed any emotion. Did the young German appreciate the way he had been portrayed by the receptionist from the Mountain Hotel? Was he annoyed by the prosecutor's accusations, as though the magistrate were speaking not about him, Werner, but about someone who had usurped his identity and taken over his entire person? But how could such role substitution be imagined? It is conceivable only in an actor. How would I have done it? Yedidyah wondered. Napoleon, when incarnated onstage, uses the actor just as the actor uses the emperor. Could Descartes be wrong? The "I" who thinks is not necessarily the "I" who is. And then who is Werner Sonderberg? Where is he right now, now that his life hangs in the balance? To what distant place, or dark region, do his thoughts lead him?

After all, though this courtroom has become the center of the world for everyone assembled in it, Werner Sonderberg, the defendant, would have a perfect right to turn his back on us, as an expression of his disdain or despair, while outside, far away, life follows its unchanging course. Storms in Chicago. Fires in Arizona. Car accidents and holdups. Deadly conflicts in Asia, Africa, and the Middle East, as though they had been programmed since the world's creation.

Guilty or innocent? Is Werner Sonderberg playing with words when he says he is "not guilty but not innocent"? What does he mean? That he's innocent but also a bit guilty? Can a person be both at the same time? How could reason accept such a thing? Could God not exist? Could it be that the angel of death no longer exists? Can he die? In the theater, who could incarnate him to make him visible? A clown maybe? Or an object? How could a director, no matter how brilliant, be able to present him in a way that would arouse in the public the terminal anguish and desperate appeal to a faith that refuses to be extinguished?

Yedidyah was saying to himself that he would have liked to interview the defendant. It suddenly seemed urgent and essential to meet him. Just as he used to make a point of questioning the character he was playing when he was studying dramatic art, he was convinced that, in order to do a good job describing the trial, he had to speak to the person who, more than anyone else, held the key to the truth. But the rules are rigid. No one can talk to the defendant while the trial is in progress, except his defense attorney.

A rush visit to the editorial offices. Kathy offered him her cheese sandwich.

"As an hors d'oeuvre," she said with a malicious wink.

"Thank you. But I prefer it at the end of the meal."

"One day, you'll be entitled to both. But first, drop by to see Paul Adler. He's waiting for you."

The editor in chief, in shirtsleeves, was on the phone. He hung up as soon as he saw Yedidyah.

"So," he said, laughing, "you're not too mad at me yet for the burden I placed on your frail shoulders?"

"And what about you, you're not too mad at me for having accepted?"

"Up to now, you've been doing well."

The two friends joked for a few minutes, then Paul became his usual serious self. "This trial has already lasted a week. Do you think it will go on much longer?"

"At the beginning, the experts said it would last about five days or so. Hard to say for certain when the curtain will come down."

"But the fellow . . . is he convincing? Where does he

belong according to you? In a Greek tragedy or a Shakespearean drama?"

"Hard to say. Is he guilty of what he's accused of? I have no idea. Is he innocent? I mean, did he play no part in his uncle's tragic death? I have no opinion. In fact, I'm completely in the dark."

"Meanwhile, I notice how influenced you are by theater. Like certain playwrights, you don't like to use the word 'crime.' You talk about passion and fate. But the court has to judge the intent and criminal act of a man who, up to now, has limited himself to making an odd statement. To put it plainly: How long will this little game of 'guilty and not guilty' last?"

"There's no way of knowing. We're now at the end of the first week. For the time being, things are going badly for the defendant. What can you expect? The jury see things in simple terms: the two men left the hotel together and only one returned."

"And how's the fellow going to explain that?"

"If he knows the answer, he's keeping it to himself. I have the feeling that something is stopping him from defending himself."

"What? Can't he come out and say he had a moment of madness, an uncontrollable impulse, had slept badly, eaten badly, had too much to drink, or something? That the old man had tried to seduce his fiancée?"

"I don't see him saying that. It's not his style."

"So what's his style?"

"I have no idea."

Paul stopped to think for a moment, then blurted out, "The man seems more and more interesting. We should find out more about him."

"I did think I should meet him, interview him. Not easy. Is it even possible? Is it allowed? What about asking a specialist? Your usual legal reporter, for example?"

Paul asked Kathy to call him. She replied that he was out of the office. On vacation. Impossible to contact.

"Contact Sonderberg's lawyers," Paul concluded. "Tell them an interview with their client could help him." Can they make an exception?

Yedidyah promised to explore the possibility.

When the hearing resumed, the judge reminded Elisabeth Whitecomb that she was still testifying under oath. She seemed a bit nervous. Or worried. Maybe she was afraid of the defense lawyer's cross-examination. Yet Michael Redford was not aggressive. In his own way, give or take a few fine points, he asked her questions to which she had already replied. Had she noticed any tension between the young traveler and his uncle? No, she said. Hadn't Werner been concerned about his older companion's well-being? No. Had she been informed, perhaps by a cleaning lady, that the two men had quarreled? No. Other innocuous questions followed, leading to the same negative responses. Then, to come full circle, the attorney asked her, "How many times did you see Werner Sonderberg at the hotel?"

"Several times. When he went to the restaurant or went out for a walk, he stopped and chatted a bit."

"What did he like to talk about?"

"About the weather. The news. The beauty of the mountains."

"What was your impression of him?"

"Attentive. Courteous. Friendly."

And the cross-examination finished with a final exchange.

"When the young German checked out of the hotel, did it occur to you that he might have killed his uncle?"

"No. At that point, no one knew that the old man was dead."

"Did you think he was capable of committing a murder?

"No," she replied after hesitating.

"Why no?"

"Why yes?"

She paused and then added, "Where I sit, at the reception desk, I greet a lot of people, men and women, Americans and foreigners. Giving them the once-over is a work tool."

"Thank you, Ms. Whitecomb, that will be all," said the lawyer, taking his seat again.

The judge was about to dismiss the witness when the prosecutor stood up.

"Your Honor, may I submit one last question to the witness?" The judge nodded yes.

He turned to Elisabeth Whitecomb.

"Of all the guests, men and women, whom you observed in your hotel, did you ever have one who was later charged with murder?"

"No," the reception desk attendant replied. "I don't think so."

The prosecutor sat down after gesturing with his hand in the jury's direction: for him, things were clear.

"Don't forget, the reader doesn't just want to watch the event, he wants to take part in it," Paul often said to me. Fine with me.

Late afternoon. I go back to the office and write up my account of the hearing. I'm not satisfied with it. Yes, I summarize the speeches of the prosecution and the defense. I describe the defendant's behavior, the ambience in the hallways, the impassive attitude of the jury, the reaction of the public. But I feel that something is missing: I'm unable to convey the feeling that an entire life hangs in the balance, with all its mysteries, and a future of infinite possibilities. One carefully weighed sentence, or one word amiss, and life can tip down on the good or bad side. A feeling of frustration comes over me as I reread what I wrote. If an actor—me?—were to read my words onstage, I'm sure the audience would start to wriggle in their seats and cough gently to hide their impatience.

Should I put an end to this experiment, ask Paul Adler to release me? I don't dare disappoint him. Should I pass the burden on to Charles Stone, head of the city desk, and let him find someone to take my place? That would be the easy way out. As my grandfather used to say, it isn't for us to begin; the beginning is the Creator's privilege. But it is incumbent on us to begin anew. So, Grandfather, if that's what you want, I won't stop midway.

Yet, I have to admit, if only to myself, that it wouldn't be my only setback. At this point I felt I'd failed in almost all my endeavors. Even with Alika, the proof being our quarrels. I feel fragile, broken. Pinned down. I wonder why. But I don't really want to know the answer.

I go over the list of my most glaring shortcomings and my mediocre triumphs. More or less docile son, more or less acceptable student, failed actor, journalist with a still clumsy pen, inferior lover, troubled husband. So much for the negative. As for the positive: a kind of sincerity, courage, and a need for lucidity. When I throw myself into an adventure, I don't accept half measures. When I love, I love with my entire body and my entire soul (though for how long?). When I have a friend, I'm completely devoted to him. I think I gave my close relatives all the affection I could. The person who most moved me? My grandfather; his image remains intact in my memory. Because he suffered? Rather because he knew how to channel his suffering and transcend it without betraying it. And my father? When I think of him, the same emotion wrings my heart. Because . . . what? Just because.

This doesn't mean that I don't love my mother, my brother, Itzhak, his wife, Orli, or my uncle Méir. I love them all, but differently. To be more precise: it is my grandfather whom I loved differently.

I recall a story that I read somewhere. A young girl is standing by the window and says to herself: I love my parents, I love my cousins, I love my friends, I love everyone except myself. It's me I don't love. And she throws herself out of the window.

This image troubles me. To chase it away, I think of my grandfather again. He never demanded anything, never asked for anything, and never expected anything from me that wasn't in harmony with the things I wished for myself in my dreams. My grandfather is a sage. Please note: I said a sage, not a saint. It is from him that I learned to be wary of saints.

It is from him that I acquired the desire to delve, relentlessly, into the secret work of Kalonymus ben Aderet whose aphorisms nourish my thought, my quest, my need to believe in the other and in my own self.

When the trial is over, I say to myself, I'll go and meditate on his grave. May he guide me to vistas where—with a bit of luck and if I can prevent my audacity from slipping away—I'll no longer be a failed person.

THE NEXT DAY, THE TAXI DRIVER who had driven Werner to the station was called to the witness stand. This was the same driver who had picked him up at the train station when he arrived. A Mexican native, surly, clearly annoyed with this courtroom business, with the loss of his time and therefore income, he didn't even look at the defendant. But he did look at his wristwatch constantly.

The prosecutor asked him if he had already met the defendant. An affirmative reply. In what circumstances?

"I drove him to the station."

"Did he talk to you?"

"Yes."

"When?"

"When we arrived at the station."

"What did he say to you?"

"Two words. 'How much?' "

"That's all?"

"That's all."

"What was he like?"

"What do you mean?"

"Was he in a good mood? Worried? Morose? Preoccupied? Upset?"

"I have no idea. I didn't look at him. Not even in the rearview mirror."

"Was he deep in thought, as if something serious had just happened to him?"

"I just told you: I didn't look at him."

Other witnesses were called to the stand: waiters from the restaurant, chambermaids, other hotel guests, policemen, inspectors, forensic scientists. But the duels between the prosecution and the defense lacked vigor and passion.

And that's when the coup de théâtre occurred that would put an end to my career as a legal reporter.

Two depositions shed a new light on the proceedings: that of the medical examiner and that of the superintendent of the New York apartment building where Werner had his studio. The dates and the facts didn't match.

At the time of Hans Dunkelman's death, Werner Sonderberg was already at his home in Manhattan.

In my last article I described the hubbub in the courtroom. The judge's furious outburst: they had wasted his time. The jury's contentment: they could return to their pleasures and occupations. The smiles of the defense attorneys. The fiancée's happiness. But also the defendant's lack of joy.

Why?

And why, when he first answered the judge, had he stated under oath that he was both guilty and not guilty?

ACTOR, JOURNALIST, WANDERER, Yedidyah did everything to give himself a direction in life, and then he tried again to find a new goal. Whatever he was doing, he liked to throw himself into it with a feeling of complete freedom. When he was writing, or taking a walk in Central Park with his two sons, he thought only of them and their future. Even when he was doing nothing, he dismissed everything else from his mind so he could be fully conscious of his idleness. In confronting his inner void, he was eager to be its center.

One day, he stood in front of the window, watching the clouds come together, drift apart, make holes in the sky, both large and small.

"What are you doing, Daddy?" little Dovid'l asked him.

"Can't you see?" his father replied. "I'm working."

"Working on what?"

"I'm studying the void."

Yedidyah explained: "In life, my son, everything has

meaning. Even things that may seem meaningless to you. But then the meaning is harder to find."

Dovid'l didn't try to understand and returned to his room.

That, too, must be in the novel.

IT MAY BE TIME TO REVEAL that my grandfather, the man whom I loved so dearly, is not my grandfather; Rabbi Petahia is not my ancestor; my parents are not my parents. Mine are dead. The enemy killed them when I was an infant. A strange story? Unusual? Not really. Literature abounds with such stories. When the Tragedy is referred to, the law of probability is scoffed at. In good and in evil, the imaginary creeps behind real-life experience. Many stories that we think are improbable and impossible are actually true. Only the details, the dates, and the names differ. The rest . . . My adoptive parents eventually revealed the truth about my early childhood.

Once upon a time, in Central Europe, in a small city called Davarovsk, there was a Jewish couple, my real parents, who led a normal life. They had two children, a ten-year-old boy and an infant, me.

My father worked with a textile dealer; my mother was a housekeeper. They were happy. I am convinced of that. I own a photograph that proves it. It was taken a short time after their wedding. They are young. And attractive. He has a serious look on his face. She has a half-tender, half-provocative smile. I imagine them absorbed in their love and in their faith. The photograph was taken when they were visiting my maternal great-grandfather. I found out that he lived in a neighboring village and was a tutor to the farmers' children. My parents are sitting under a blossoming tree. Smiling. Do they believe in eternal love? I think so; I hope so. Such things weren't flaunted at the time.

An old Jew from the same town remembered them. I met him by chance at the Yiddish theater in Manhattan. I don't recall how we began talking about Davarovsk; perhaps because of the play. It was about life in Brendorf, a small town, a now vanished shtetl among many, engulfed in the maelstrom of the Tragedy. "I'm from Davarovsk," the old Jew said to me. I gave a start. My heart began racing. Had he known the Morgenstein family? I asked him. The textile dealer? Yes, of course. And what about Wasserman, was the name familiar to him? Yes, it was, he remembered him. A man who was always calm, almost withdrawn. He had married a girl who was a great beauty. My interlocutor continued speaking, but I no longer could hear anything. I was suddenly choked with emotion. Fortunately the bell rang, announcing the end of intermission.

The fate of my parents and grandfather? As might be guessed, the same as that of so many other Jews. The ghetto. Fear. Hunger. My mother's suffering: How was she to feed her husband and two children?

I think of them often, I confide to them my secret fears about the state of my health, I try to imagine how they lived out their last hours, and I feel like weeping, and hiding in order to weep more freely. But then I'm afraid I won't be able to stop.

So I, too, lived for a time in the Davarovsk ghetto. Probably until it was liquidated. My adoptive parents explained this to me; they knew much more about my early days than the old man I had met at the Yiddish theater; he had been deported in the penultimate convoy. That's how my real name was revealed to me: Wasserman. I wish I could put it on my parents' tomb in heaven.

But how was I saved? Oddly enough, I don't owe my survival to a powerful lord or a dedicated humanist, nourished on moral principles, but to the innocent and sublime soul of an illiterate peasant woman, a decent, humble Christian from a humble nearby village who took care of me when I was born and helped my mother with the housework. Maria. Gentle Maria. That's what they called her in my house, as I later learned. From then on she, too, would not leave my thoughts. Was there a way for me to summon a recollection of her? Some psychologists would claim that she is still buried in my unconscious; if they're right, I'd like to find a way into it; perhaps I'd discover the traces she left there. Maria's age? One elderly survivor describes her as svelte and youthful; another younger one says she was short and old. Did she have a family? Yes, of course. But she never spoke about them. It seems that she sent all her earnings to her parents. Devout? She often crossed herself. Even to bless me? No doubt. She went to church on Sundays. Taciturn, not very talkative. Sweet and, above all, honest. And loyal. Courageous in the face of danger? Let's say intrepid, resolute.

It was her idea to separate me from my parents. One night, a few days before the deportation, she succeeded in entering the ghetto and came to see her former employers. She offered to protect our house, if necessary, from robbers and vultures. They gave her permission. They trusted her. She then made a more surprising suggestion: that they entrust me, their baby, to her. Did she have an inkling of what would eventually happen to them? In our little community, though there were frightening rumors going around, no one knew. But she thought I might get sick from a long trip to an unknown destination, for as it was I was excitable, sensitive to the cold, and frail. She swore on her own life and on Christ's that she would watch over me and look after me. They would get me back, safe and sound, as soon as they returned.

Did they have a long discussion? Doubtless it was difficult and painful. Did my mother cry? Maybe. I imagine she did. Was my father the first to give in? There's no way of knowing. But Maria's logical reasoning and tenderness won the day.

Maria took me home to her village and introduced me as her own son, though she wasn't married. Hence, I was suddenly illegitimate. The father was said to be a drunken soldier who subjected her to horrendous physical abuse one night before leaving for the front. Did I suffer from losing my mother's warmth and my father's love? I really don't know. Nor do I know whether Maria's parents were brutal in their treatment of her or me. Did they punish me for the "shame" she had brought on their family? Everything I later learned about them filled me with bitterness and outrage. Maria was as magnificently kind and tender as her parents were ill-tempered, morbid, and cruel. They saw me as an intruder.

I found out that shortly after the war, Maria took me to a big city where the agents from a Jewish charity were looking for Jewish children who had been hidden by Christians with compassionate hearts, while others tried to find adoptive Jewish parents for them. That's how I came to America. My "parents" at the time knew only one thing: my name, which was written on a piece of paper by my father and given to Maria. Now that my "American parents" have given it to me, I never part from it: it's my personal treasure. An unexpected discovery: I thought I was the child of survivors; I'm not. I'm a child survivor. In fact, I ought to mention this to Dr. Feldman. My past might explain my health problems. And then what? I decide to wait.

Both outside and inside, I bear my paternal great-grandfather's name, Yedidyah Wasserman. I cherish a photo of my real parents.

Understandably, I wanted to track down Maria by every means possible. Not easy. I didn't know her last name. I had only one desire: to go there. But how could I know if she was still alive? And if she was, how would I identify her? I opened my heart to Alika, hoping to appease the animosity she had been showing me since the Sonderberg trial. To my amazement, she encouraged me to make the trip, even if nothing were to come of it. That way, she said, you won't be able to blame yourself for not having tried to thank the woman who made it possible for me to meet you. And she smiled faintly. Had we finally reached a truce?

So I returned to my native Carpathian town of Davarovsk. Thanks to the photograph of my parents, I succeeded in finding the street and the house where we had lived, or rather the two-story building that had been built on its ruins. When I saw it I felt something between an immense void and a bottomless, nameless grief. Later, I would try to explain it to Alika: "Imagine a character, onstage, feeling pain, anger, and fear, who wants to cry out and make the walls shake; he opens his mouth but remains frozen and mute for an interminable moment. Tell yourself this was me, as a tiny child, probably frightened, in front of what had been my house with my parents and their plans at the time, the shared hopes my brother and I embodied."

I spent only a few hours in that small town. Occasionally a passerby came up to me, intrigued; he wanted to know what I was doing in his street. My guide, young, self-confident, and secure in his position, replied with a few words in Hungarian or Romanian. Satisfied or not, the man would shrug his shoulders and go about his business.

After a sleepless night spent in the only hotel in town, I pursued my pilgrimage to the out-of-the-way village where I was told I might find the woman to whom I owed my survival.

An old peasant woman. Ageless. Silent. Sitting on a bench in the public gardens under a blossoming tree. Motionless. Emaciated face, scored with wrinkles. Gazing into the emptiness.

It is she. The guide made enquiries—at the neighbors', at the town hall. Maria Petrescu. Once the maid of the Jews in the big town. Heart of gold, soul of a saint.

I tell the guide to ask her if she remembers my family. She doesn't answer. He repeats the question. Still no answer. The door of a wooden house, right near the gardens, opens and a peasant, about forty years old, emerges. He comes up to us, looking unfriendly.

"What do you want?"

"Nothing bad," the guide says, reassuring him.

"Then go away. Leave her alone."

"We'd just like to ask her a few questions."

"What questions?"

"It's personal."

The peasant becomes irritated. "Don't you see that she can't answer you?"

"Why?" the guide asks.

"Because she can't, that's all. She no longer has all her wits about her. She lives in her own world. We have to force her to eat and drink. What can I say? These things happen. We want to live, grow old, then time goes by. We're here but not she."

I feel a pang of anguish. I had arrived too late.

"A shame," says the guide.

"Why a shame?"

"Because we have gifts for her. And money."

"Gifts? For her? For Maria Petrescu?"

"Yes. For her."

The peasant seems lost. He doesn't understand. Nor do I. Something about this situation, this moment outside time, escapes me. She saved my life and now I should be able to save hers. Except it's too late.

"I might be able to help you," says the peasant after hesitating. "I'm her nephew. Vlad. Vlad Petrescu."

I ask the guide to briefly explain to him the reason for my visit. The nephew doesn't look surprised. He had heard that a long time ago his aunt had lived far from her family. But he doesn't know with whom. Did he know that during the war, she had been close to a Jewish family? That she had saved their younger child? No, he'd never heard that. Did she ever marry? No. Never. But . . .

"But what?"

"People in the village said things about her. Every place has its share of contemptible, nasty people."

"What did they say about her?"

"Oh, silly things. That she had led a shameless life. That she had had a lot of lovers."

"Where? In the village?"

"No, of course not. Here everyone knows everyone else. People said that in town she gave in to her instincts. That she was beautiful and a slut. That men ran after her, which wasn't surprising. They even said . . ."

A pause. The guide eggs him on.

"What?"

"That she had a child."

"A child?"

"A little boy."

He lowers his voice and adds, "A bastard. Obviously, since she had no husband."

I hold my breath. I glance at Maria from time to time. Can she hear us? Can she understand what her nephew is saying about her, about her life? Here was a courageous, honest, honorable woman, a credit to the human race, and she was treated with contempt! How are we to live in a world where values are so perverted? Where human feelings are so devalued? And yet, fortunately, Maria Petrescu exists: if Christians no longer frighten Jews, it is thanks to her. But how she must have suffered! Moving and magnificent heroine.

"But I'm forgetting," the peasant says. "You mentioned gifts. For her. Why?"

The guide turns to me, hoping I'll suggest an answer, but

none comes. A heavy silence sets in. Vlad scratches his head for a moment, then cries out, "Wait. I have things to show you. They come from my aunt."

He quickly walks away from us and, after quite a long time, returns holding a large envelope.

"This is what remains from her youth," he says.

My guide seizes the envelope; instinctively at first, I don't dare touch it, as if it contained a corpse, the corpse of an extinguished memory. But then I examine the contents of the envelope. A faded, yellowed identity photo. A lovely oval face, a modest gaze, a reluctant look before the camera. Yes, she was beautiful, the woman who rescued me. I no longer dare look over at the old, tired, motionless body.

Another photo: a house with a garden. The nephew explains. "This is where she worked during the war."

Our house. Mine. I'm seeing it for the first time. How was it furnished? How many rooms did it have? How many closets? Beds? Was it joyful inside its walls? Were my parents happy before misfortune struck them?

A last photo: Maria with a curly-headed little boy. He is clinging to her skirt.

"This was her son," says the nephew. He makes a vague hand gesture. "We don't know what became of him. They say that his disappearance made her ill. She no longer wanted to see anyone. See that barn there, behind you? That's where she used to take refuge. To sleep. To shed tears in silence. They say she grew old quickly."

I go up to her, by myself. I search through my distraught,

worried memory. Where in there is she hiding? How deeply would I have to dig to find a memory of her? What can I do to make her rediscover me, make her react to my presence, to elicit a gesture, a gleam in her eye? I try to catch her gaze. Empty. A wall. I touch her arm. She lets herself be touched. I smile at her. I whisper my name in her ear. Then hers. I tell her I'm pained for her. That I feel close to her. That I'll remember her. I tell her the secret that I've been foolishly hiding from everyone, even from Alika, and my friends, and my children: that I'm sick. I reassure her: I'm alive and I'll stay alive. Has she heard me? Her lips part, but no sound comes from them. Has the well run dry? A tear appears in her right eye. And in the left one. I kiss her gently on the forehead. She falls back into her lethargy.

The nephew seems puzzled.

"What about the gifts?" he asks, as if to break the silence.

I signal to the guide to give them to him.

"Tell him to swear on everything he considers sacred that he'll take good care of his aunt."

Astonished, the nephew vows to take good care of her. Twice.

I leave Maria's village, and then the town where I was born. My heart is heavy: I am leaving behind a stolen segment of my life. Should I have gone to the cemetery? An old, gray tombstone surely bears the name of a great-grandfather: Yedidyah Wasserman.

Should I have come sooner?

When was sooner?

"YOU WHO EMERGE FROM THE DELUGE where you were drowned, when you speak, remember your weakness in the dark times from which you escaped," Brecht writes.

And the journalist wonders: Who escaped? Me?

And what about my big brother, that unknown little boy?

Vanished without leaving a trace. Swept away in the storm of ashes that ravaged History and cast a pall over it forever after. This is something I think about, too, from time to time. Why weren't my parents able to find a safe place for him? It must not have been easy. The good Maria no doubt tried, but who could give him a home? Not her parents at any rate, on whom she was already imposing a baby they hated. Why would they have taken on the added burden of a ten-year-old Jewish child?

Yedidyah thinks about this "big brother," just a doomed little boy, and he feels overcome by a violent emotion. He doesn't even know his name. Was he tall or short? Timid or bold? Cheerful or melancholic? Studious or lazy in school?

Brilliant perhaps? In mathematics or music? Did he have school friends? The only thing his younger brother knows about him is that his life went by like a shooting star. He was ten years old when he died over there, in the kingdom of oblivion. He remained with his parents—their parents—to the end. Should he envy him for that? You can't envy someone who is faceless.

Who can he blame, who can he hold responsible for his death? A naive question: How could the survival of a Jewish child, who didn't have the time to experience happiness, threaten the world's equilibrium? A less naive question that he never asked his grandfather, unfortunately, and that was never raised by the great Rabbi Petahia: What about God? Under what name was this child listed in anticipation of the Day of Judgment by the man who keeps the Book of Life and Death open during the High Holy Days?

Yedidyah wrote to the Davarovsk municipality. They must have kept a birth register. Disappointment: a few months before the liberation, a Russian bomb had destroyed the archive wing.

It is as if this older brother had never existed.

Was this possible? Even for God? Did he sometimes give life in order to immediately erase it? Why? Yedidyah had no idea. But he discovered one thing.

That it was possible.

The following thought is attributed to Voltaire late in life: "Happiness? Happiness is living and dying unknown."

With his whole being, Yedidyah cried out: he is wrong, the great French philosopher is lying.

After returning home, like a man possessed in quest of an elusive truth with multiple masks, Yedidyah set out on a pilgrimage to his family's origins. He devoted all his free time to it, encouraged by Alika, even though she didn't fully understand this new obsession.

First he focused on books. After all, this was the easiest path. He consulted the archives at the resource centers, reference libraries, and museums devoted to the memory of the Holocaust in Washington, Paris, and Jerusalem. The records dealing with "hidden children." Niny Wolf and Judith Hemmendinger in Alsace, the Zionist Sruli Rosenberg in Haifa, and Rabbi Benatar in Bnei Brak. A priest in Toulouse, a physician in Strasbourg. All these utopians with compassionate hearts who scoured Europe as soon as the war ended, with just one goal: to return the Jewish children saved by Christians to their parents if they were still alive, or to the Jewish community if they were not. How and where could he find these exceptional, exemplary men and women? He was advised to consult lists; there must have been some. There were. But Yedidyah didn't know how they could be useful to him: he was missing too many clues. He slept badly, worked badly, lived badly. He was often in despair but refused to become resigned. Sometimes he felt close to suicide. Why? For no reason perhaps. Out of boredom. To escape from the inner emptiness that defied him and made him dizzy. In order to accomplish an act that would be his own beginning and his own end.

One night, Alika woke him. He was moaning.

"Why don't you try hypnosis?" she suggested. "I read an article about it somewhere. A psychiatrist who can revive old, distant, buried memories. It wouldn't hurt you to try."

Alika finally located the man, actually not such a rare bird: therapists and psychiatrists who use hypnosis are not difficult to find in New York.

A young athlete, suntanned and with a clear gaze, greeted Yedidyah and, to the latter's surprise, requested that he take a seat facing his desk rather than recline on the mythical couch so valued by followers of Freud. Professor William Weiss seemed pleasant and likable.

Second surprise: "I know your name. Yes, I've read your reviews. Theater is somewhat of a hobby for me. I could have become an actor, but—like you, no doubt—I prefer to watch and listen. However, I like your approach to theater. You don't come across as a burned-out actor or an unlucky playwright, but as a lover of the stage; someone who refuses to consider himself defeated and finds his own way of expressing his love of beauty, art, and artistic truth."

They spoke about theater for a while until finally the professor said: "But I'm sure you didn't come to see me in order to discuss the latest production of the great and incomprehensible Jason Palinov. What brings you here this morning?"

"Memory," Yedidyah replied.

"I see," said the psychiatrist. "Are you having problems with it? Do you think you're losing it. Is it playing tricks on you? You can't remember where you left your pen, or your car keys? Afraid of Alzheimer's, is that it? All intellectuals are afraid of it. But you, you're still fairly young . . ."

"That's not the problem," Yedidyah said, embarrassed.

"What is it, then?"

Yedidyah explained his case to him. Repressed memories for which no clues remained. He couldn't remember his early childhood. He could rack his memory, scour it, coax it: to no avail. It was wrapped in an opaque veil. In his very first memories he saw himself on a boat. He must have been about four years old. He was part of a group of children all about the same age. He was later told that this ship had brought him to America. He could only remember that he had become weak. He slept, and when he woke up he found himself in a family that had become his own.

"What language did you speak?"

"Yiddish."

"Not English?"

"English, too. I don't know how I managed, but I don't think I ever learned it. It's as though I've spoken it all my life. But this is not my reason for being here in your office, Doctor. I don't know who I am, or where I come from. My name was changed; I feel I'm someone else and therefore betraying the child I was and the man foreshadowed in that child. It's as though I were living a lie, Doctor. That's my problem or, if you prefer, my ailment. And I'm told that under hypnosis everything that's hidden away might be revealed to me. Am I mistaken? Am I deluding myself? It seems to me you're my last hope."

Professor Weiss smiled and explained to his visitor that things were not so simple: hypnosis, he said, doesn't necessarily have the same effect on all patients. For some, its effects are a long time coming, while for others they're almost instantaneous. For obscure reasons, there are still others who resist it, remain distant, and then the therapist is simply powerless.

"But we can try," he concluded.

"Right away?" Yedidyah asked, a bit frightened nevertheless.

"No. Next time."

After some last-minute hesitations, Yedidyah made an appointment.

Luckily, Yedidyah did not resist hypnosis. He let himself be willingly and pleasantly guided by the therapist's voice, which was at the same time neutral and controlling. It doesn't feel like he's sleeping, or even dozing, but rather like he's dreaming. He sees himself in a pretty little city; there are small houses, gardens in bloom, many trees, many birds under a gray and stormy sky. But the streets are empty. The houses, too. Everyone is hiding. Yet the little boy is not alone. A man and a woman are holding him by the hand as they go down into a dark basement. He's shivering; he's cold. He knows they love him, and he loves them, but he also knows they'll abandon him. So he starts to cry. And the woman takes him in her arms and kisses him, while whispering in his ear, "Don't cry, my darling baby, my beloved, you mustn't cry; you're a Jewish child and Jewish children have no right to cry. You must live, you must, you're all we still have on this earth. Promise me you won't cry, promise me you'll live."

"And then?" asks the therapist's faraway voice.

"Then nothing."

"Nothing?"

"I want to cry. With all my heart I want to cry. But I don't."

"And the woman? You're little and you're in her arms . . ."

"Yes, in her arms, that's it."

"She's your mother."

"I'm in my mother's arms."

"And the man?"

"He, too, he takes me in his arms."

"He's your father."

"Yes. I'm in my father's arms."

"And then what?"

"Then nothing."

"And no one?"

"Yes. A boy. He reads books. When he reads, he doesn't talk."

"Who is it?"

"My brother."

"His name?"

"Dovid."

"Dovid?"

"Dovid'l. I love him. He plays with me. I make him laugh."

"Who do you see?"

"People. In the street. In the courtyard. In a garden. But they're nothing. It all amounts to nothing."

"These people, do you know them?"

"Strangers. I don't like them. They're mean. Brutes. I don't know them. I don't want to know them. I want them to go away. I want them to let me go away. They're there because my father isn't there. Because my mother isn't there. They scare me. Scare me so much that I ache. I ache all over. But I keep silent."

"These people, what are they like? Tall? Short? Fat? Well dressed?"

"I don't know, I don't want to see them. I see them without seeing them. My father left me because of them. My mother abandoned me because of them. I'm cold now that she's no longer with me. I'm always cold."

"These people don't warm you up?"

"They're nothing to me."

"Do you sometimes see yourself as happy over there?"

"Yes. With Dad and Mom."

"Do you sometimes laugh over there?"

"Now that my brother left me, I don't laugh anymore. I see myself in the empty basement of an empty house, and the empty house is located in an empty city. I see myself there and I know that I'm empty, too."

Yedidyah admits to Alika that this trip inside his memory distresses and disorients him.

"A name, recall a name."

"Over there, I have no name. I'm too little. I'm not entitled to one. I'm a Jewish child. Jewish children have to rid themselves of their names so they can live."

"The people in the basement, what do they call you?"

"When they come, they motion to me. I obey."

"And you, what do you call them?"

"I never call them. They call me. To eat. To drink. To sleep."

"Do they hit you sometimes? Do they punish you?"

"Yes. No. They're abusive. Bad tempered. They never smile. I feel threatened. Threatened when they're absent. And when I see them before me."

"When you have an ache somewhere, what do they do so you'll ache less?"

"Nothing."

"Do they speak to you?"

"They yell and I hear nothing."

"And when you're sick?"

"I stay sick."

"No physician has come to see you?"

"No one has come. Ever."

"Are you often sick?"

"Yes, but I don't say anything. My parents forbade me to talk when I'm not well. It's no one's business; that's what they said to me."

"So how do the mean people know?"

"They don't know anything. They don't love me. I'm a hindrance to them. They hate me. They resent me for being there, alive, in their house, in their life. The last time . . ."

"The last time what?"

"The last time I was sick it was like I was drunk. I saw things. Intruders. I saw my dad. Behind him, I saw my mom. They motioned to me not to say they were there. All of a sudden they disappeared. Slowly. First their legs disappeared in a cloud. Then their chests. Their necks. Their heads. Everything turned white. And as red as fire. Thick. Thick ash. I knew it was a dream. I was sinking. I started yelling, but no sound came out of my throat. I yelled louder. Louder and louder. I was yelling in silence. My lungs were bursting; I was reeling; I no longer knew where I was. Or who I was. I woke up later, very late. On the boat. There, too, I knew it was a dream, though I wasn't sure that it belonged to me or concerned me. Perhaps I had simply changed dreams."

Professor Weiss says something, then his voice falls silent.

Yedidyah tells him a story that he got from his aged grandfather. It was a few days after his parents had revealed to him the secret of his birth.

"Once upon a time there was a young Jewish boy who lost his father. Naturally this deeply affected him. He never stopped sobbing all day. Even at night he sometimes shed tears in his sleep; he would wake up drenched from head to foot. 'What makes you grieve so much?' his mother asked him on a day when he seemed particularly unhappy, so much so that he couldn't concentrate on a difficult passage in the Talmud. 'What hurts most,' replied the boy, 'is not being able to follow in my father's footsteps. How can I hope to resemble him, for he left too soon for me to benefit from his teaching? How can I become the second after him?' And his mother reassured him: 'In that case, my child, tell yourself that it was written up there that you would not be the second but, in your own way, the first.' And my grandfather added: 'This little boy became the founder of a Hasidic dynasty.' "

"So what's the moral of that story?" Professor Weiss asks.

"I have no idea," replies Yedidyah.

"Nor do I. But it seems to me we can see it displays a definite dose of optimism. No doubt your grandfather wanted you to understand that you, too, in your own way, could become a kind of first."

Yedidyah thinks for a moment.

"The other little boy had the luck of growing up with

his mother; I didn't. In fact, I pointed this out to my grandfather."

"And how did he react?"

"He found me a bit unfair because, he said, after all, I have parents who love me just as if their own blood flowed in my veins."

"And you replied?"

"That there's no comparison. That it isn't easy to live a life that is partially mutilated. I'm convinced that if I could get my childhood back, I would feel better. That's why I'm counting so much on you, Professor."

Yedidyah breaks off. He takes a deep breath as if to free himself of a burden. Then he starts talking again. "In fact, I couldn't help telling my grandfather that I'm convinced I'll see my parents and my brother again. In the other world, the world of truth. And with a sad smile my grandfather asked me, 'And what will you do with us, over there?' I answered, 'I'll introduce you all to one another.' Help me to stand fast, Professor. Help me to make headway in reviving my extinguished memories."

Professor Weiss said he would do his best.

When he went out into the street, Yedidyah had a thought, as he sometimes did, for Werner Sonderberg: Is it possible that he, too, would have been happier, twenty years earlier, if he had been able to extirpate from his memory a grief that had colored his life?

TROUBLED AT THE TIME by the vague feeling that his life or the meaning of his life had escaped him, Yedidyah was on the verge of despair. He came close to becoming a mystic. He was no longer himself. Restless, nervous, hypersensitive, constantly irritated. Unbearable. In doubt about himself and his ties to Alika. He suffered through long nights of insomnia and self-questioning: Since I'm not the man I thought I knew, who am I? Asceticism of silence and rejection of all desire that drove Alika crazy. He couldn't understand his own ineptitude: How could he not have guessed the truth, or at least not partially suspected it? He was angry with himself. He had lived and grown up among strangers whom he called Father, Uncle, Grandfather. He loved them as though they shared the same past. And now, of course, his own children were perpetuating this lie by calling his parents Grandfather and Grandmother.

Alika tried in vain to reason with him.

"Think about what you owe this family that became ours, that took you in with limitless generosity, with unconditional love, never denying you anything. Try to be grateful for our luck, our happiness. You could have ended up with heartless and distant people. We both know we've met unhappy adopted children. And also men and women brought up by their real parents and yet unhappy for a host of reasons that escape us."

"That's a good argument," Yedidyah answered in a tense voice. "But you're wrong if you think I'm mad at my 'parents.' I'm mad at myself. For not having been able to figure the truth out sooner."

Unsettled, distraught, his soul shaken, Yedidyah kept searching stubbornly for the "tree of life and knowledge" on which he could have leaned while confronting the intoxication of the unexpected. But he was burdened by his thoughts as others are by their bodies. They caused him to become morose and bitter.

What would have become of him without the innocent gaze and sadness of his two children, who, being young, didn't understand his mood swings?

AT NIGHT, HALF AWAKE, FEVERISH, I sometimes talk to my dead brother.

"I miss you, you know."

"I don't know."

"But I do. I made you laugh."

"That's good. But you don't know me."

"Not my fault. And you, do you know me?"

"Of course. We talk about you often, Dad and me."

"You're with him?"

"We're together."

"Since when?"

"Since always. We made the trip together."

"In the leaded freight car?"

"Yes. In the dark. We were suffocating. Mom sang a song for me."

"Which one?"

"My favorite lullaby. A prince and a beggar love the same girl. The girl loves beggars, so the prince leaves his palace to become a beggar."

"A sad story."

"For whom?"

"For the king?"

"But kings are never sad. Only princes are."

"I'm sad; and I'm not a king."

"So become a prince. What are you waiting for?"

"Me, too, I prefer beggars."

"I believe you."

And after a sigh: "What's your name?"

"I'm not allowed to tell you. Where I come from, beggars have no names."

Alika wakes me. "You're crying in your sleep."

On another night, I speak to my dead father. "I want to see you so badly, but you're far away."

"I'm not far away."

"So why can't I see you?"

"Because my world is not yours."

"I envy my brother; he's with you."

"But we're with you. We're you."

"Tell me a story."

"A child is crying. He can't stop crying. A sorcerer tries in vain to make him laugh. An angel tries to make him dream, in vain as well. God takes pity on him and makes him see the invisible and hear the inexpressible, and the child answers Him: since You're so powerful, see to it that I stay with those who are absent."

Alika pulls me out of sleep. "You're moaning again."

On yet another night, I speak to my dead mother. "Help me, please."

"You're suffering, my child. Tell me everything."

"I don't know anything about you anymore."

"What do you want to know?"

"Show me your face."

"I can't. It's forbidden."

"Forbidden by whom?"

"By the good Lord."

"Why?"

"I don't know. Perhaps in order to separate the living from the dead."

"But I don't like this separation!"

"I don't, either. But we can't do anything about it. Neither you nor I."

"Did you love me before . . ."

"Before what?"

"Before abandoning me?"

"Before saving you, you mean. Yes, I loved you. I loved you gently, passionately for the rest of your life."

"Did you kiss me often?"

"All the time."

"While talking to me?"

"While whispering words of love in your ear."

"In silence, too?"

"Yes."

"Kiss me, Mom."

"I'm not allowed."

"But you love me, you just told me so."

"I love you, my child."

"Then kiss me once, just once."

"No."

"Why not?"

"Because I want you to stay alive."

Alika shakes me. "What's happening to you? You're delirious."

Suddenly, I don't know why, Jonas sprang to mind. The imperious editor of our editorial pages, he was perhaps the wittiest member of the staff. He hated his work; at least that's what he claimed. All these people, he grumbled, who hold definitive and irrevocable positions on everything under the sun and beyond, it behooved him to correct them and censor them. A cynic, he resented them for foisting the role of bad guy on him. He kept complaining about this morning, noon, and night. Under the circumstances, why didn't he request another position, I asked Paul. Because he was the only person who could do this thankless work without fearing his victims' revenge, said Paul. Jonas wrote badly, but he knew how to help others write well. In the same way, he made people laugh, often through self-mockery—though he himself never laughed.

On the day he announced his retirement, the editorial

staff responded with a warmth he didn't expect. He was convinced that everybody hated him.

We weren't friends, but I invited him for a drink in the café across the street. I ordered a coffee and he a brandy. So early in the morning? A matter of habit. Could he be an alcoholic? No, a need to warm up. He's always cold. A second brandy. He must be freezing. And for the first time, I noticed a sadness about him that made me feel ill at ease. And then I suddenly realized that I didn't know anything about him: I didn't even know if he was married. How could I question him about his private life without offending him?

"Listen, Jonas," I said to him, "I have a suggestion. Why don't we meet again tonight for dinner? Alika sometimes has her head in the clouds, but she just might surprise us with an excellent meal."

He thought for a minute. I expected to be turned down. "My wife is waiting for me," or some such thing. After all, we'd never been close. To sound him out gently, I added, "Feel free to bring someone."

"I'll come alone," he said after hesitating for a long time. "But not to your house. I prefer a restaurant. And promise me not to speak about my old work or my plans."

I felt like adding "or your wife," but I restrain myself.

"I promise."

We dined alone. Alika had gone to the theater and the twins were sleeping over at my parents' house.

After a few banalities about the noisy ambience of New

York restaurants, the weather, and journalism's overall decline, there was a long silence. Jonas seemed embarrassed. Why did he accept my invitation if he didn't really want to come? The reason became apparent when he said, "At the time, I read your stories on the Sonderberg trial."

It was already the distant past.

I expected devastating criticism, but instead he launched into a didactic analysis, at the end of which he said that he considers the defendant guilty.

I couldn't help retorting, "What about the plain facts?"

"The facts have nothing to do with it. I'm not saying the young German killed his uncle. I'm just saying he's guilty."

"If he didn't kill him, what is he guilty of?"

"Guilty of having abandoned a man who was going to die."

"But how could Werner have known that ahead of time?"

"Maybe he should have."

I told him I disagree. You can't blame a person for not being a prophet or a psychologist. A man is guilty only if he has actually killed someone. And suddenly I realized that Jonas's lips were trembling. Was he sick? I fell silent. So did he. The food before us was getting cold. Then he started talking about Albert Camus. Of the fear this writer arouses in him.

"You might have read his novel *The Fall.* The story of the judge who blames himself. He had witnessed the suicide of a young girl in Holland. That was really all. But he was there. That was enough. Could he have intervened? Probably not. But he was present. He saw. Hence his guilt."

I felt like pointing out to him that Werner's uncle was all alone when he died, too far away for anyone to see him; at any rate, his nephew wasn't with him. But Jonas continued: "Your young German also saw. He was actually the last person to have seen his uncle, yet he left. His departure is an act that implicates him. An act that had the value of a judgment. He condemned his uncle to solitude. Hence to death. To suicide."

Here again, I was about to tell him he's too strict and unfair and, whatever he may think, Werner may have decided to leave the old man precisely so as not to pass judgment on him. But once more he silenced me with a hand gesture.

"For Camus, the choice is between innocence and guilt; for me, it's between arrogance and humility. The question is not whether we are all guilty, but whether we are all judges."

"Are we judges, you and I?"

After pausing for a moment, he said, "I was one."

Jonas told me of a dream. He was in the lobby of a hotel. At night. He saw a rather beautiful woman walk toward the exit. She seemed depressed and unhappy. Jonas was surprised by one thing: she didn't have a purse. Only a kind of envelope in her hand. Where could she be going? To meet a lover? The next morning they knew: she had gone to meet death. They found her under a tree, with the empty envelope next to her. Jonas broke off and I was about to ask him if he felt guilty when he woke up, but I didn't dare. Jonas lowered his head to avoid my gaze.

"It wasn't a dream. It was a nightmare."

That was all. He didn't say anything else. Nor did I.

Today, I think about his words again: "We are all judges."

But then, as our sages wonder, who will judge the judges?

FINALLY, THE MEETING WITH Werner Sonderberg. He and I and his Anna are in the lobby of his hotel, not far from Times Square. Travelers come and go. At the bar, guests are talking and laughing; we could be at a fair on a summer evening. I immediately ask him the question I'm sure he was expecting.

"Why did you want to see me?"

"To see you again," he corrects me.

"Very well. See me again. Why?"

After a pause, Werner suppresses a smile before replying in a sober but tense voice, "You wanted to see me again, too. Am I wrong?"

"Not really . . . but in the past, yes, during the trial. Then it was too late. I didn't think it was possible."

"Why not?"

"It all seems such a long time ago."

He exchanges glances with Anna—as though he were consulting her: Should he be frank with me or prevaricate? A good couple. A real one. Their complicity is obvious.

Everything he knows, she knows, too. Their marriage and the years have changed them. That's normal. Earlier, at the time of the trial, they weren't married yet. He seems both more solid and more vulnerable. When he was before his judges, before the media, he always seemed absent. Not anymore.

"Personally," he goes on, "I wanted to see you because I read your newspaper reports at the time. And during the entire proceedings I wondered whether you thought I was guilty. Your articles take sides. You hesitated, you had your doubts. I found this—how should I put it?—morally interesting. Remember, I was a philosophy student at the time; for me, everything was related to metaphysics. That's why I wished to meet you. But what about you? Why did you want to meet me?"

"I was puzzled by your attitude. 'Guilty and not guilty' may be an acceptable answer for a philosopher, but not as far as the law is concerned. The judge explained it to you. But for me, your refusal to choose reflected the most serious problem man can confront: that of ambivalence. In the tradition I belong to, it isn't an acceptable option. Since you were innocent, why didn't you say so plainly? You would have spared yourself quite a bit of trouble. You would have benefited from doubt. Some people among us were ready to believe you from the first day."

"First of all," Werner immediately replies, "I never considered myself innocent. I said guilty *and* not guilty. From the standpoint of the truth, this 'and' was important. And do you really believe that everything is crystal clear in life? That it's always this or that, one or the other: good or evil, happiness or sadness, fidelity or betrayal, beauty or ugliness? You're not that naive. Admit it, a clear-cut choice, so distinctly drawn, would be too easy, too convenient."

What could I say in response? What he said isn't wrong. Purity is legitimate only in chemistry. Not in the intrigues of the soul.

Once again, Werner looks at Anna questioningly: Should he show all his cards, exchange them for new ones, or just stop the game? His attitude reminds me of my first years with Alika: whatever we did, we both wanted to do. We acted under the same impetus. Werner makes up his mind. He leans toward me.

"What if I told you that Hans Dunkelman was not my uncle? Would you be surprised?"

"Yes, I have to say I would be. But I'd be most surprised by the fact that you hid this information during the trial. That served no purpose. The question wasn't whether Dunkelman was your uncle or someone else, but whether you were the person who killed him."

Werner looks at me for a long time before adding in a lower voice: "It was he who had changed his name. And you'll understand why: Hans Dunkelman was my paternal grandfather. His name was Sonderberg."

Though I didn't know why, this confession moves me. Perhaps because it makes me think of my own grandfather.

"Okay," I say. "So you didn't kill your 'uncle.' But,

knowing he was your grandfather, would you have killed him more deliberately?" I ask sarcastically.

"Perhaps," he says, looking at me fixedly.

"What? You're joking . . ."

Should I point out that the joke is in bad taste? He doesn't let me finish my sentence.

"We quarreled. Violently. In his room, as soon as we arrived at the hotel. And again on the third day, when we went for our walk in the mountains."

I understand that a serious event must have taken place. Now it's my turn to lean toward him.

"You quarreled. Fine. That happens to everyone. There are people who spend their lives bickering. With their fathers, their mothers, their spouses, and their in-laws. But what was your quarrel about?"

I look at Anna who turns toward her husband and encourages him to answer. I ask them if I may take notes. They have no objections.

"About hatred," Werner replies. "Our quarrel revolved around hatred. A bitter, fierce hatred, kept alive by death, entirely turned toward death: How could it be overcome? For it has to be overcome if men want to continue living in a world to which they are still condemned. That's the conclusion I'd come to on that day: I wanted to hate, wanted to hate hatred so I could triumph over it. I had to, but everything within me refused to succumb to its call."

He starts to tell the story he should have told at the

trial—not so he could have proved his innocence, but to have given truth a chance to be victorious.

When Werner went to the bathroom, Anna lowered her voice and said to me, "So you can fully understand what you're about to hear, it's important for you to know that he lost his father a short time before the trial."

"From disease?"

"From cancer. Grief and everything that goes with it."

She cut herself short as soon as her husband joined us again.

So here is what had happened in the tall, dark mountains of the Adirondacks.

The two men had gone there not for a vacation but in order to have a heart-to-heart talk. About the past. "Things" from long ago. Protagonists from a story that will shame humanity until the end of time. There was something unreal and timeless about their confrontation. In their one-to-one encounter, the two men represented the two faces of the worst species, the one called the human species.

Yes, Hans had been a member of the Nazi Party. Worse: he had been an SS officer. Worse still: he had been a member of the *Einsatzgruppen,* the special commandos whose task was the annihilation of every last Jew in occupied Europe. He had changed his name because he was on every list of persons wanted for crimes against humanity.

"Don't ask me how it happened or why," he said to Werner. "I know why, though you'll never know. I mean, you'll never understand. A defeated Germany, on her knees, pitiful. And me, too. Young but withered, scorned, poor, and famished. Humiliated and miserable."

Hans described the First World War with disgust, "lost because of the Jews and their Communist allies." The enemy within. The famous stab in the back. The disastrous Versailles Treaty. The smallest new state became more important, wealthier, more respected than Germany. The Weimar Republic: Hans called it the laughingstock of nations, cowardly, pernicious, open to all perversions, to all concessions, rushing headlong into bankruptcy. You had to fill a suitcase with banknotes just to buy a pair of shoes or a piece of bread. People sold entire buildings to foreigners so they could get by from day to day. In respectable families, fathers avoided their children's gaze. Everyone felt their country was now the dregs of the civilized world.

Then Hitler entered the stage. He alone knew how to say the words that the people wanted to hear. Hans became impassioned: "By naming the guilty—the Jews, the Communists, the Democrats, the Freemasons, in other words, the others—he freed us from our guilt, our weakness, our defeat, our shame." Pompous slogans? Certainly. Hysterical shouts? Yes, absolutely. Threats? Yes again. Moving words, grandiose appeals to the national honor and unshakable patriotism? Yes, a thousand times, yes. "Cause trembling instead of trembling": being a penniless young man, Hans had to believe in this slogan in order to believe in the future. So the Third Reich became a religion and Adolf Hitler its prophet if not its god.

"Can you imagine yourself in my place, at that time?" Hans asked. "For us, this was a matter of learning to walk tall again, head held high, singing of the glory of death of whom we were the proud and faithful allies."

"How do you expect me to respond?" Werner said. "In the course of my studies I learned one word I'll never let go of: 'Why?' If I had been in your position, I think, I hope, that at each stage I would have wondered: Why? Why the threats? Why the repression? Why the prisons? Why the camps? Why the massacres? But I wasn't in your position."

"No, you weren't."

The weather was beautiful amidst the trees in the mountains. A gentle, light wind caressed them. A golden sun played with the docile earth. In the distance, in the valley, you could make out a town and the gray and red tiled roofs of the houses. A rural ambience, too peaceful and benign for the blows and wounds the two men were inflicting on each other.

"I suppose you're only at the beginning," said Werner. "Do you want to continue?"

"The pride of putting on the black uniform of Heinrich Himmler for the first time. Of being accepted and feared. Of fulfilling special missions for the Führer, so admired and so loved: a spiral or escalation, the orders and actions progressed in boldness, brutality, and cruelty. The Night of the

Long Knives. The books thrown in the flames. *Kristallnacht:* ah, the looting of Jewish shops; the synagogues set on fire; the old Viennese men forced to clean sidewalks with toothbrushes; others running away like frightened animals; the beauty of these spectacles swelled the young breasts of the followers."

"And the idea that your victims had harmed no one, that they were innocent—this didn't disturb you?" Werner asked.

"They were Jewish, hence guilty."

"Guilty of what?"

"Of being born Jewish."

"Therefore?"

"Therefore they had to be punished, eliminated, pitilessly—all of them."

"And it never occurred to you that they were human beings like you and me?"

"Not like you and me. They were Jewish, not human. In fact," Hans added, "it was a sight to see them, terrified and cowardly, as they were chased out of their houses, or in the camps, in Dachau and later in Auschwitz, emptied of life, emaciated, like walking corpses. Not just the Jews, but their accomplices, too, their political allies, their business associates or accomplices in God, their sympathizers, pathetic humanists of all stripes. Up until then, they had wealth, enviable positions, titles, important jobs: we took off our hats to them; we almost went down on our knees to greet them. With our treatment, they started crawling on the ground like animals to pick up a piece of stale bread or a cigarette butt. Not the slightest trace of dignity, or pride, or even anger. They didn't belong to the same species as me."

"And what if I told you that even then, even over there, those you assaulted, those you humiliated were still as human as you? Though pitiful, these men and women had preserved their humanity by weeping, while you lost the very last speck of yours? Can you understand that?"

"You're the one who doesn't understand. You weren't in my position."

"I never would have agreed to be in it."

"Are you sure of that?"

Hans let out a kind of momentary laugh. Werner found no hint of bitterness in it. Then the old man asked, "Between owning the whip and being subjected to its lashes, you would have chosen the lashes?"

"I hope so."

"In that case, I think this conversation is useless. You'll never understand."

"Understanding implies an equality of standards. I refuse that."

They looked at each other with harsh severity. With the same violence? Was one the exact reflection of the other? How can the impact of gazes be measured? Anna was becoming increasingly pale. She was in agony hearing about this conversation between the grandfather and his grandson. She was speechless.

"Keep going, get to the end of what you wanted to tell me," Werner said.

"What else do you want to know?"

"You mentioned Dachau and Auschwitz."

"I was there. Dachau first. Compared to what came later, not too terrible. I obeyed orders. Humiliate the prisoners; weaken their resistance; take away all their willpower. Kill their humanity, their hope. That was the main objective. They had been brought there to strengthen and glorify the Nazi ideal. While showing respect for German law and those who administered it. The prisoners had to understand this intangible truth and permanent reality: they were tools in our hands; when they became useless, they were thrown away."

"But you were a tool, too, a malleable tool in the hands of your superiors. Their excesses, their bloodthirstiness, their mind-numbing blindness didn't disturb you?"

"It's not the same."

"In what way?"

"I don't know. Let's say that at the time, it didn't occur to me. Actually I didn't think about anything. My leaders thought for me. My duty was to obey. To serve a cause that I knew was sacred. Eternal. It justified all undertakings. Even what you call our monstrous crimes."

"Yes, that's what I call them."

"You believe that I, your grandfather, was and still am a monster?"

"A human monster, or inhuman, it makes no difference.

And the fact that I'm your grandson is unbearable to me and makes me boil with indignation; there's a part of me that refuses to accept it."

Suddenly wounded, Hans's face took on a cold, distant expression.

"So that's it. You reject me. Though you haven't heard it all yet."

"I'm ready."

"So listen closely," said Hans. "Kamenetz-Podolsk and the Hungarian Jews, Kiev and the Ukrainian Jews. Vilnius and the Lithuanian Jews. Barbed wire as far as the eye can see. Huge communal graves. I saw. Shattered heads. Infants pummeled, scorned, trampled, used as targets. I saw. The undressing sessions. The stupor of women pushed into the gas chambers. Silent old men with stony shattered faces. I saw. What did I feel? Nothing. I felt nothing. The gun I held, I was that gun."

He became ironic, cruel. "You, darling little grandson, you would have gone mad. With rage? With pain, no doubt. Whereas I felt nothing. I was Death. You're Death's grandson."

He broke off and his cold gaze penetrated Werner's, seeking to hurt him. "What you've just heard is merely the beginning. You have nothing to say to your grandfather about this?"

"One more question: You never felt any remorse?"

"Never."

"Regret?"

"Yes. Even today I still regret having lost the war. We could have and should have won it. But history never stops. The final victory will be ours."

"You killed. You assassinated. You massacred. And your only hope is that this horror recurs. You changed the world into a huge spectacle of ugliness, sadness, desolation, ash, and now you tell me this taught you nothing. That the future will resemble the past. And yet I'm still your grandson."

"Do you want me to stop talking?"

"No. Continue."

"Say: 'Continue, Grandfather.' "

"No."

"What do you mean 'no'?"

"It's time someone had the courage to say no to you."

"You're not the first person. Your father said no to me. Shortly before his death."

"I'm proud to be his son."

Hans frowned.

"In spite of what I told you, you won't recognize any extenuating circumstances in my case?"

"No, none. Even if you felt remorse I'd be against you."

"In that case, you asked for it. Should I go on?"

"Go on."

"Treblinka and its columns of smoke. Birkenau and its ovens. The gas chambers. The whistle of the night trains arriving directly at 'the ramp of the Jews.' Promoted officer, I supervised the selections, the gassings, the shootings. Day after day, night after night, hour after hour, impervious to the tears, lamentations, despair of the victims, death was dealt ruthlessly, efficiently, with talent and dedication. It was simple and implacable: in this cursed place, the condemned had come to die and I had come to kill. At no time was I seized with remorse or pity. I saw everything, I retained everything. I thought it was necessary. That it was just."

Motionless, horrified, Werner cried out angrily, "And you want me to be proud of being related to you?"

"Whether you like it or not, you are. By blood."

"Well, blood can lie. In our case, it lies. You and I, we don't belong to the same human family."

"There again, whether you like it or not, we're related; we're relatives."

"Then I'll bear this kinship like a burden. Worse—like a curse."

Hans sniggered once again. "You're like your father."

"What's he got to do with it?"

"Isn't he the link between us?"

"Of him I'm proud. Whereas you make me sick."

Werner was overcome with a rush of loathing; he let it sweep over him, but his gaze didn't detach itself from Hans's.

"Will you ever come to understand what you did to me and to my generation? Hitler and you, you kept proclaiming it was for the future of Germany's children that you were at war with the rest of the world; for us that you were destroying entire cities; for us that you erased our right to pride, honor, and hope for centuries to come. Before his suicide, Hitler, in his will, expressed his wish to punish the German people by turning Germany into a mountain of rubble. But what you did is worse: you took revenge on us, your descendants. Because of you, all of you, though we were born long after your atrocities, we feel guilty. Because of you, my joy will never be unmitigated. Because of you, the child I see in his mother's arms makes me think of the children you sent to their deaths. Because of you, I'm banned from the pure and powerful happiness to which all men should have access. According to a Jewish saying, life is a wheel that never stops turning. Look at your life: what you did to the Jews is what you are living through now. You wanted to isolate them, you're isolated; you wanted to hunt them down, you're hunted; you made it impossible for them to live without anxiety, now you'll never live without anxiety. And you'll share the fate of your master. For the Jews of occupied Europe, the continent narrowed to the size of a country; the country narrowed to a city; the city to a street; the street to a house; the house to a room; the room to a basement; the basement to a freight car; and the freight car to a concrete, sealed shelter ensuring the effectiveness of the gas. And their lives ended in flames. Isn't that what also happened to your Führer? His gigantic Nazi empire began to shrink: the continent was reduced to a country; the country to a city; the city to a street; the street to a bunker—and he, too, was consumed by flames."

Hans's face had turned ashen. But Werner went on.

"Shall I tell you something else? My father died of a cancer, but it is you who killed him. He couldn't bear your hatred of all things noble in the world. Clearly, he knew everything about you. He knew you were a fugitive. Knew that you deserved society's contempt, and prison, if not something more drastic. Your son regretted being born, regretted being the fruit of your seed; the cancer that undermined him was the 'you' he had inside him, the memory of you, of your blood and your past. And now you're so brazen as to think I'll forgive you? If that's the case, you're crazy."

Hans, transfixed, suddenly seemed frightened. Werner wondered by whom or by what: Was he afraid of the truth, or of being hunted and alone in the world, in the midst of a humanity that repudiated him?

"Yet," he said in a hoarse voice, "I loved your father. I had other children, but he was my favorite. It was he I chose to be my heir. He was everything to me. It's because I was thinking of his career, his future power, his conqueror's destiny, that I took the path you abhor; it was in order to brighten this new era with pride, a pride unprecedented in the history of the human race, that I donned the black uniform. Yes, it was for him that I was intent on following Adolf Hitler and supported his plans of extraordinary conquest and glory. I wanted your lives to be pure and strong like a black diamond. Your father didn't want to believe me and now, like him, you, too, refuse to understand."

Werner was unable to control his indignation. "So it's for me and my father that you slaughtered Jewish children and their parents in the Ukraine and Poland, for us that you tortured and tormented thousands and thousands of martyrs! You repel me! And it's disgust with you that generated the illness that was to kill my father! I hold you responsible for his death!"

Then the old man completely lost his composure. His body began to shake, his face turned pale, and his grandson wondered whether this was the effect of lost dignity or of rage.

"You were my last chance, maybe my last pride," Hans whispered.

"You were mistaken," Werner replied. "I repudiate you. I disown you. In my own way I disinherit you. I extirpate you from my life; I erase you from my memory."

The old man shriveled up; his face darkened.

"So you're saying I fought for nothing?"

"You fought for hatred, for evil and death."

"That's all you have to say to the German patriot I've always been? And that I'll always remain?"

"Yes. That's all. I pray that God will remove you from my path forever."

"So I lived for no one," Hans stammered. "And for naught."

On the horizon, the sun had yet to set. A stronger wind shook the trees. Hans stood up and turned his back on his prosecutor and judge. Werner walked away from him with a heavy tread and offered him not even a farewell glance.

His grandfather's death wasn't a murder but a suicide, Werner told me. The autopsy revealed that he had had a lot to drink. Had it been an unintentional fall? Possibly. Perhaps Werner was responsible for his grandfather's decision, consciously or unconsciously. Perhaps not.

So: Guilty or not guilty?

WHAT DID WERNER SONDERBERG expect from me? Did he want me to comfort him and provide him with the arguments with which he could forgive himself? But for what crime, what offense, what mistake? Didn't his tormented conscience testify to his innocence? And why had he chosen me as his confidant or confessor? Did he want me to tell him that if I had come across his grandfather in those days, I wouldn't have survived? That he would have shot or gassed me, without giving it a thought, when I was a month or a year old, so as to enrich the hypothetical existence of future generations of Germans?

Suddenly, the image of my own "grandfather," the descendant of Rabbi Petahia, loomed before my eyes. So generous, so human. He knew how to deal with his own suffering and bereavement; but what does one say and do for other people's? What advice would he have whispered into my ear? That I show empathy for the assassin's grandson, he, too, a victim of the Nazi curse?

I gave Anna an embarrassed smile and looked at her husband with a sort of melancholy, as I understood that, in a sense, I had been luckier than he. I could think of my relatives without shame, whereas he had to keep struggling to free himself of his past and find a modicum of peace, if not happiness, in life. Wasn't it my duty to help him rather than keep him at a distance? An old Hindu text was suddenly called to mind: sometimes the earth, collapsing under the burden of passions and the fear of its inhabitants, asks the gods of all humanity for forgiveness.

Overcome by a strange emotion, I did something that I had never done before: I started talking to them about my grandfather.

But I don't remember which one.

When I returned home, I found Alika in tears.

"Dr. Feldman called; he wants to see you tomorrow."

I then felt oppressed by a muted anxiety: the medical exam of a week ago. I'd never thought about it again.

Tomorrow is yesterday in Israel. Should I warn my two sons?

The doctor was both optimistic and preoccupied. The news wasn't disastrous, but it wasn't particularly good, either.

I have an enemy in my body. War has to be waged against it. Bah, I'm used to it.

THOUGH I DIDN'T KNOW IT, for a long time I was an orphan, Yedidyah said to himself. Actually, I have always been one. And now that I know this, how can I continue to live the same life as before? How am I to let my sons know that, for some time, their father has loved them more and more? That he's felt closer to their mother? That, yes, the grandparents they had loved so much had actually been strangers, but that they must love them, too? What more is there for me to do or undertake in this cold, cruel world in which, superficially, I am linked to so few things, so few close relatives, for they themselves are tied to a person who isn't me? A faint glow lit up in my mind: What if I surrendered to the nihilist impulses that every man harbors in his heart? Or, on the contrary, what if I devoted my remaining years to helping others who feel they should track down their buried memories, seek out living ties, the branches of one same oak? Running until I was out of breath, ripping off masks but consoling bereaved souls, seducing seducers, laughing with old men and crying with children, stealing from the thief, seeking serenity in one place and fervor in another? For a prisoner of fate, who dreams of freedom and solidarity, isn't being present a sufficient motive for saying yes to humanity?

Yedidyah remembers: for reasons, at times obscure, at times crystal clear, he often wanted to be elsewhere, to run away. He wanted to go somewhere and return to an unknown past and an elusive imaginary world where someone could tell him what life was: An escape? An imposture? An error?

No, he was not going anywhere, at least not yet. Everything in its own time. He couldn't abandon his home, his wife, Alika, the mother of his children, his "parents," his "brother," his "uncle," the memories of his "grandfather." But how is one to live inside quotation marks?

Under a cloudy, rainy sky, he sat under a tree where he often went when he was young to reflect about his more or less chimerical theatrical ambitions; he opened the diary that he kept assiduously in those days and read:

Odd. In everyday life, I see myself onstage; and on the stage, I'm plunged back into the everyday. So where am I?

And now, sitting at the kitchen table while Alika is sleeping or pretending to sleep, he keeps turning the pages, then stops at random.

Alika and me. Méir and me. Antigone and Creon? No. Antigone and me. Godot and me. Ulysses and me. We belong to the same species. Ultimately, from one man to another, the fate is still the same. I speak to them, they answer me. I speak for them, as though I were the other in them. Is all this normal? It's theater. On the boards, we all belong to the same family.

He looks for a blank page and writes:

Suddenly I don't understand anything anymore. Why life, why death? Would the latter be the only truth and the former a sham?

I no longer understand men and their Creator: Do they share the same goal? A long-term plan? At least an initial meaning? My grandfather believed in God, believed that the tie between the Creator and His creation is the fruit of a common intent and will, an integral part of the work they had undertaken together. But what is that tie? Is man condemned to advance toward death because he is God's victim or orphan, or because he is His partner?

I don't understand the march of destiny. I no longer understand the hope of the living or the language of the dead.

I don't know why the good Lord thought it good or useful to create this ever so complicated, unpredictable, mixed-up, and contradictory human race.

I don't understand what I'm doing among men, all of whom are orphans or will be one day, or why or how I belong to their community.

I no longer know anything, since I am nothing. Could Ecclesiastes be right? Could a living dog be better than a dead lion? Is it preferable and more sensible to visit a house in mourning than a tavern? Was Job wrong to make peace with his God though the latter had delivered him, without telling him, into Satan's hands merely so he could win a bet? Vanity of vanities? Everything is vanity? But then, what the devil should we do about our rumors, our desires?

Why am I here rather than somewhere else?

Why am I me, whereas I could not exist, or I could be another?

The years go by and leave moments like scars. Angst and hope persevere in their tireless struggle.

Yedidyah is worried, troubled: he has understood that he might not have much of a future: he is no longer young, his memory is feverish, his body has trouble withstanding the weight of the years. What will the doctor say tomorrow? How much time does he still have ahead of him? How is anyone to know? Do we ever know? An assessment? Not yet. This applies to Anna and Werner, too. We don't live in the past, but the past lives in us. Sooner or later, man rejoins those who preceded him. His two sons will live their lives in the Holy Land: there, too, one day Jews and Muslims will learn to build peace. And Alika? Her passion for the stage will not die down. She'll continue on the path she mapped out for herself. She will have to choose her parts, her friendships. She will forget.

Is the life of man a tragedy, or a farce with no real beginning or end? Is it the Creator's sin or error? The memory of a memory, the dream of a delirious fit? Wise Men compare it to a speck of dust, a leaf fluttering in the wind, a world in ruins. Fine, I accept the lesson, as a warning. But have I made mistakes? Errors? Who pushed me to make them? To prove what? Isn't a failed destiny still a destiny? In any case, in the end it will be fulfilled. God is patient, says the Koran. God is silence, says a medieval Jewish mystic. God is. He is in the wait.

In the meantime, the point is to live the truth every instant. To hope, so that others will hope in turn. The hours will be added to the hours, the nights to the nights, the masks to the faces. The sun will not be snuffed out and the blind, regardless, will walk in their darkness. God and Satan will continue to quarrel over the souls of men. As for Yedidyah, he will string words together. The angel with countless eyes will wait in the wings. The soul keeps its own chronology: Can one choose one's previous history? One's roots? The "father" becomes Dad and the "mother" Mom. God alone does not change. There is only one path known to a human being who lives in time: to live in the present using up all his resources, all his resilience. To make each day a source of grace, each hour an accomplishment, each wink of the eye an invitation to friendship. Each smile a promise. So long as the curtain has not fallen, everything remains possible. Somewhere on earth, each person is acting in his own play; here or there, it makes one or another stranger weep or roar with laughter. Their link is the poet's reward. Is life a corridor between two abysses? A Wise Man makes this suggestion. But then, what is the good of putting in an effort? One way or the other, eternity is contained in the instant that vanishes.

In that, Yedidyah takes after his grandfather.

He is no longer alive. Nor are my parents. I'll remember my grandfather's funeral till the day of my own. He had made me read his will: contrary to the American custom, he wanted to avoid funeral orations, reduce them to a bare minimum. And above all, the circumstance should not be used to "celebrate his life," as they say here, by telling funny stories. For a dead person, it is not funny. Dignified, sober, and sad, such was his funeral. As I left the cemetery on Alika's arm, I felt that a part of me had been ripped away.

One of his remarks, recorded a few days before his death, has taken on a new meaning for me:

> Yes, my child, life is a beginning; but everything in life is a new beginning. As long as you're alive, you're immortal because you're open to the life of the living. A warm presence, a call to action, to hope, to a smile even in the face of misfortune, a reason to believe, to believe in spite of setbacks and betrayals, to believe in the other person's humanity, that's called friendship.

There's the secret of what we so inadequately call the life or destiny of man.

But he knows that, if you believe the old sages, when a just man dies, God weeps and makes the heavens weep. And their cries reverberate in the immensity of the ocean. Then it is given to His children to gather the tears from the stars in order to water the heart of the orphan, forever open, in spite of everything, to an impossible joy, always searching for a reunion, at long last, with his real departed parents, who were not characters in a play.

A NOTE ABOUT THE AUTHOR

Elie Wiesel was fifteen years old when he was deported to Auschwitz. He became a journalist and writer in Paris after the war, and since then has written more than fifty books, fiction and nonfiction, including his masterwork, *Night,* a major best seller when it was republished recently in a new translation. He has been awarded the United States Congressional Gold Medal, the Presidential Medal of Freedom, the rank of Grand-Croix in the French Legion of Honor, an honorary knighthood of the British Empire, and, in 1986, the Nobel Peace Prize. Since 1976, he has been the Andrew W. Mellon Professor in the Humanities at Boston University.

A NOTE ON THE TYPE

This book was set in Old Style No. 7. This face is based on types designed and cut by the celebrated Edinburgh typefounders Miller & Richard in 1860. Old Style No. 7, composed in a page, gives a subdued color and an even texture that make it easily and comfortably readable.

Composed by North Market Street Graphics
Lancaster, Pennsylvania

Printed and bound by RR Donnelley
Harrisonburg, Virginia

Designed by M. Kristen Bearse